Love at First Doubt

Love at First Doubt

A BAD BOY COWBOY / CURVY GIRL ROMANCE

ROUGH & READY COUNTRY
BOOK ELEVEN

ENGRID EAVES

Prologue

EFFIE

"There's a dead man in my bushes."

I don't know why I whisper. The only creatures in earshot are a mother cat and three kittens I'm fostering. And I live alone in the cul-de-sac of a historical neighborhood populated with nineteen-thirties Craftsman homes and bungalows with ample space between.

"A dead man in the bushes? Are you certain?" the overly chipper male dispatcher asks. I may be a sunshiny, optimistic morning person. But even I have my limits when it comes to cheerfulness. Fielding a call about a cadaver in the landscaping is one of those.

"Am I sure?" I ask, knitting my brows and thinking out loud. "He's not moving, and considering it's a pyracanthas bush, yes, I'd say I'm sure."

"Pyracanthas bush? What's so special about those? Are they poisonous or something?"

"You haven't seen one of them before? They're the big decorative bushes with bright orange berries... Now that I think about it, those berries very well could be poisonous..." *Did I mention I get overly chatty when I'm nervous?* "Anyway,

1

they have very long, very painful thorns. So, I'm pretty certain the only way a body would end up lying in one is if they're stone-cold dead. Don't you want my address or anything?"

"Thanks to the miracle of modern technology, we've already traced your location, and I have the sheriff en route."

"Nice..." *for a podunk mountain town.*

"Hey, did you happen to check the man's vitals?"

"God, no," I sigh exasperated into the phone. "I'm not going anywhere near that body. What if he's like a rapist or a murderer or something?"

There's a long silence on the phone. Finally, the overly happy man replies with a smile still twinkling in his voice, "Ma'am, a dead rapist or murderer won't pose a problem."

I don't know if this guy just wants to dick around with me or what, but I'm over it. "Please don't tell me you want me to confront a dead body at seven-thirty in the morning. It's still kind of dark outside."

"No, my no," he says, laughing into the phone. "But I have to ask. You know, just in case."

"Alright, well, I'm not going anywhere near the guy."

"Totally understandable. Would you like me to stay on the line until first responders arrive?"

As much as the chipper guy annoys me, he also represents a lifeline. "Yes, please."

"By the way, my name's Paul. So, what have you been up to this morning besides finding dead bodies?"

"I was up early playing guitar and singing. I have a whole slew of Halloween songs I'm getting ready for Hollister Elementary School's Fall Harvest Program. I'm Josephine Jackson, the new kindergarten teacher..." I don't tell him that the Halloween song playing quickly turned into jamming and belting out some of my favorite rock tunes at the top of my lungs...

My eyes tick to the bush. Did I just see the corpse's

cowboy boot twitch? I shake my head and rub my eyes, gawking at the legs. *Don't let your imagination run away with you, Effie.* It loves doing that, which is a huge plus as a kindergarten teacher and an even bigger minus as an adulting twenty-something.

"Oh, nice. My—"

"Oh my God!" I exclaim, my voice jumping a full octave and quavering at the end.

"What?"

"He's moving!" I half-whisper, half-scream, shivering uncontrollably.

"Oh, good for him," Paul replies.

"Good for him? How much longer until the sheriff gets here?"

"Should be any minute. I called the ambulance all the way from Ophir City, though. Do you think we're still going to need it?"

"I don't know." My eyes round as I watch the man sit up. Besides boots and jeans, he's got a black cowboy hat covering his face, which he stiltedly removes to run a hand through his brown hair, long on top and shaved on the sides, like an unstyled mohawk. He places the Stetson atop his head, glancing around. The muscles ripple beneath his tight-fitting Social Distortion T-shirt with the short sleeves rolled up, and everything from his neck to his arms, hands, and fingers are covered in colorful tattoos. He rests his head in his hand for a long moment, and I hold my breath, stuck between panic and admiration.

"I don't mean to jump to any conclusions, but would it be safe to say the man is no longer dead?" Paul asks sarcastically.

I exhale sharply. "I can tell you really enjoy your job, Paul."

"And?"

"And, yes, he appears to be alive." He also appears to be ridiculously handsome. His jaw is angular, his face square-cut, and his nose long, straight, and well-proportioned. A short brown beard covers his cheeks, which may be more like a couple of days-worth of afternoon stubble, and his body is broad-shouldered and lean with a tapered waist. Lithe is the best word to describe him, like a dangerous, feral cat. After the second shake of his head, he jumps to his feet with an explosion of athleticism.

Turning his back to me, he tips his head forward. *Wait, what's he doing?* The breath strangles in my throat.

"Are you okay, Ms. Jackson?"

"He's peeing in the bushes," I stammer.

"Like right now?" Paul asks.

"Yes, right in front of me."

"Well, stop watching, Ma'am. The guy needs his privacy."

I hiss, "A man sleeps in my hedge before peeing there, and I'm getting called out?"

"When nature calls, nature calls. Besides, I don't get the impression you'd let him into your house to relieve himself."

He has a point.

"Oh!" I take a step back from the kitchen window. "He just turned around, saw me, and waved. And now he's heading towards the back slider." Despite waking up in bushes, the man moves with a masculine grace that embodies the "Stray Cat Strut."

"Are his pants zipped up?"

"Yes, thankfully."

"Good. At least he's polite, and we won't have to worry about indecent exposure charges." The front doorbell clings, making me jump.

"I think the sheriff's here," I gasp.

My heart races at hollow rapping on the back sliding door as I see the man shield his face with his hand, squinting inside the kitchen towards me with a grumpy smile. He points to the slider's lock.

Yeah, right. Who does this guy think he is?

Rushing for the front door, I pull back the curtain, registering a blond, good-looking, clean-cut man in a tan and black uniform and a white cowboy hat. Hollister may not be my kind of town, but it's populated with plenty of cowboy-hat-wearing, tall drinks.

"The sheriff's here, Paul. Thank you."

"Good luck, Miss," the dispatcher replies, and I press the red end call button.

Opening the front door, I exclaim, "Thank God you're here. The man's not dead after all. But he's trying to get in the house."

"Ma'am," the gorgeous sheriff grumbles with a tip of his hat. "I'm Sheriff McLeod. And your name?"

"Josephine Jackson."

"Alright, Ms. Jackson, I have some questions for you. But first, let's meet your Lazarus."

"My Lazarus?" I squeak.

"Yeah, the guy who resurrected from the dead to burglarize your home."

"Burglarize might be a little strong," I correct, my cheeks darkening. "He's knocking on the kitchen slider, to be exact."

The tall, bronzed officer frowns. "I thought you said he was trying to break in?"

"Sometimes when I'm nervous, I exaggerate," I admit.

He tips his hat toward the entry to my house, and I realize I haven't invited him in yet.

"Yes, please come in. He's this way..." I stop halfway through my sentence because the sheriff's decisive strides communicate previous knowledge of this place. His cowboy boots thud on the linoleum of the kitchen and dining area floors as he crosses the distance, unlocking the slider and letting the tattooed cowboy in.

"So, this is your bum? It figures," the sheriff spits, leaning back on his heels.

"Don't ask," the man grumbles, looking toward the dining area and then me. On closer inspection, I notice minor cuts and some bruising on his face, including a swollen bottom lip. Nothing major but the kind of damage that comes with a fall or maybe a fistfight. His piercing turquoise eyes sear into me without hesitation—the rudest, most intimate glare I've ever experienced. My breath catches in my throat.

"I like what you've done with the place," he says, narrowing his gaze.

I open my mouth to speak, but no words come out as he regards me slowly and sensually, from my Marilyn Monroe-style curly haircut in ebony to my black cat eyeliner, red lipstick, button-down, black Atomic tiki cardigan sweater over an Eagles T-shirt, vintage pencil cut blue jeans that end a few inches above my ankles, and leopard-spotted Chucks. I love sporting a vintage look with an edgy rocker vibe. Although I can't read my Lazarus well, he seems unable to take his eyes off me.

He swallows hard, blinking a few times and scrubbing his eyes with his palms as if he has double vision. With a sweep of his hand, he adds, "The decor is cute if you're into that frou-frou girlie shit. But I draw the line at garden gnomes. They were eye-balling me when I woke up. It was creepy as hell."

"'Creepy as hell,' says the guy who used my backyard as his personal bedroom and bathroom?" I sputter.

He shrugs. *The audacity of this guy!* Turning toward the sheriff, he questions, "What are you doing here, Bro?"

Bro?

"I'm here to arrest you for trespassing and indecent exposure," he growls, looking at me. "You've made a great first impression on your new tenant, dumbass."

"Tenant?" My voice goes up a whole octave. "Wait, you're

Rockwell Landry? You're my landlord?" *There's no way! Rockwell Landry is an esteemed elderly man's name. Not that of a crazy, punk-looking, tattooed guy.*

He stands nearly a foot taller than me, which isn't difficult at my diminutive, though plus-sized, five foot four inches, and every part of him is gloriously lean and hard. He's no bodybuilder, but he obviously does hard labor to stay in shape, as the cowboy hat and boots may confirm.

"Please call me Rock. So, you're Josephine Jacobs?"

"Jackson," I correct. "But I go by Effie."

"That's right, Jackson. Sorry, it's been a long night." His gaze exudes a possessiveness and presumption that doesn't match a first meeting. But then, what would I expect from a bush bum?

Despite his apparent dereliction, something about the naughty half-smile on his lips tells me he's used to getting what he wants from women. The lean, muscular man stretches to his full height, his arms outstretched like a cat in the sun. Desire shivers down my spine.

Speaking of cats... Muffin and Cinnamon tumble into the room, followed by the runt, Twinkie. Rock takes one look at them and grimaces. "What in the hell?"

I shrug, smiling thinly. "I'm fostering them for Three Nations Animal Shelter. It's temporary."

"What part of 'no pets allowed' don't you understand?" A deep, resonant growl comes from the man's chest. Now, I'm certain he's part puma.

"Probably the same part you don't get of no public drunkenness, trespassing, or pissing on landscaping," Sheriff Christian grumbles.

"It's my property," Rock counters throatily. I hate to admit it, but the gruff sound does crazy, melty things to my insides. So does the sizzling look he sends me as if to say *mic drop*.

"That's not how the law sees it," Christian counters, and I nod confidently with him, though neither man looks at me.

"It is if I serve her an eviction notice for violating her tenant contract. How in the hell did 'no pets' get interpreted as three cats? Unless there's more?" The lanky guy scowls at me, his jaw muscles working overtime.

I wince. "Four. I'm fostering a mom and her babies."

"Not anymore, you're not," he fumes.

Christian laughs. "You're out of luck on this one, Bro."

"How? It's in the fucking contract," Rock says, his voice pulsing with anger.

"Good luck breaking the news to Roxy that you're messing with one of her foster placements."

My head bobbles back and forth between the two men. Roxy is the bubbly, twenty-something Native American woman who owns Three Nations Rescue. I contacted her a few months back when I got the job offer at Hollister Elementary School, ready to lend my fostering services. Only after the fact did I find and fall in love with this adorable little artist bungalow with its no-pets clause. "How do you know Roxy?" I ask breathlessly.

"She's our sister-in-law," they answer simultaneously, glaring at each other.

Is all of Hollister related?

As if the room wasn't seething with enough angst, the mama cat, Cleo, pounces into view, catching Christian's and Rock's eyes.

"Motherfucker," my Lazarus exclaims.

"It seems like you two are at a bit of a crossroads here, and as fun as it is chatting with you both, I have better things to do while I'm on the taxpayer's dime. So, can I safely assume nobody's pressing charges?"

My eyes flicker to Rock's, and my cheeks heat.

"The cat situation is entirely unacceptable. But considering my behavior this morning, I guess you could say we're even. This better be temporary, though." He motions angrily at the kittens rolling around playfully as Cleo grooms herself, purring.

The sheriff frowns, looking at me. "That's the best you're going to get out of him, Ma'am. He's a disagreeable asshole. That said, he's also your landlord and a decent, upstanding citizen despite his unconventional early-morning antics. As much as I don't feel like vouching for him, I have to because he's my foster brother. That said, are you comfortable with me leaving?"

I shrug, nodding almost imperceptibly as the corners of my mouth turn down. I'm going to have to be with how inbred this town is. The sheriff related to the town drunk who's also my landlord...

Out of the blue, Rockwell Landry narrows his eyes, furrowing his brows and channeling a James Dean vibe that makes my heart race. His Adam's apple bobbles in his throat as he says in a smooth voice, "Hey, do you have any Band-Aids lying around? I think I took a couple of thorns to my back and neck."

"If you don't mind cartoon characters," I squeak, working hard to keep my cheeks from steaming and drool from dribbling down the sides of my mouth. "They're in the bathroom. I'll be right back."

I talk and point at the same time as I shuffle down the hallway, scolding myself for awkwardly melting in front of the bad-boy cowboy. But he's got sexy desperado written all over him. As much trouble as I know bad boys are, it doesn't make me any more immune to them. Rifling through the medicine cabinet, I marvel at the man's luck. The bathroom's one of the few areas of the house more or less unpacked.

"Goodbye," I hear the sheriff call as he leaves. "No more playing dead, Bro."

Reappearing in the dining area, my eyes bug out of my head as Rockwell pulls off his T-shirt, revealing a carved, well-defined torso and chest, back, shoulders, and arms covered in more colorful ink—mostly Sailor Jerry, vintage vibes interspersed with some hyperrealistic portraits. The move is nearly as inappropriate as his earlier antics outside but far more appreciated.

Rushing forward, I push the stack of cartoony Band-Aids into his hand, jerking away quickly to avoid bodily contact. Still, sparks from his flesh dance on my fingertips. "You weren't joking when you said cartoon characters. Hello Kitty?" he chuckles, glaring at me grumpily.

"Yep," I exclaim, breathlessly. "I am a kindergarten teacher, after all." The man already knows this because I had to fill out paperwork for a credit check and employment, so I don't know why I'm restating this or why my eyes keep slipping and sliding across his bare skin. Taking a deep breath, I say, "I know this is technically your house and all. But you need to go. Because I need to go. It's time for everyone to go."

He frowns in a sensual, laidback sort of way that makes my heart bellyflop into my stomach. "But how will I reach some of these injuries on my back? They're tough to get." He turns, making the muscles in his middle back ripple as I see a few offending red spots.

Steam builds in my head until I feel like I could explode. "I'm not a nurse, and I hate the sight of blood." I lie about the blood part, but I need to stop the crazy feelings this man stirs inside me before I do something stupid. Lust, lust, and more lust fog my head and make my body twitch. "So, bye. Thank you. Nice to meet you. Whatever."

"Alright then," he chuckles lazily, his eyes crinkling at the edges before swaggering towards the front door, his T-shirt and the Band-Aids bunched in his hand, standing long and lean like a young version of Mick Jagger or David Bowie.

"Nice to officially make your acquaintance, Josephine. And thank you for the morning serenade. I half thought I'd died and gone to heaven hearing you, but then I realized angels probably don't sing The Red Hot Chili Peppers and Lynyrd Skynyrd up yonder..." He nods towards the sky.

My heart stops in my chest.

"By the way, I'm not around much. So, whatever you want to call this." He makes a swirly motion with his pointer finger that melts me like a chocolate bar over open flames. "Won't happen again. In fact, I doubt you'll see much of me...if ever... unless you renege on your promise and try to make the cat thing permanent." He cocks his head to the side, scrutinizing me for a long moment. "Or you get a bee in your bonnet to call the cops on me again." With a somber look and a wink that couldn't contradict each other more, my Lazarus disappears, and I shut the front door, propping myself on the interior side, catching my breath...

Chapter One

EFFIE

TWO MONTHS LATER

I pull my black leather jacket and white and black knit skull scarf more tightly around me to ward off the wind's biting cold, entering The Human Being, clutching the latest in a steamy cowboy romance trilogy in my matching mittened hands. *Is it wrong that I picture the hero in the book as my Lazarus? Probably.* But it's also safe.

Rockwell Landry might be a bum and a grump, but he's also a man of his word. I have never seen or heard from him again. At first, I anticipated his return, which helped speed along getting Cleo and her kittens adopted to good, deserving homes. But as the weeks turned into months with no sign of him, I relented, offering my services to Roxy again, which my mom thinks is the stupidest thing in the world.

But what are the chances of Rockwell Landry showing up passed out in one of my bushes again? Besides, I've since looked up the law regarding landlord entry on a tenant's residence, reassuring myself he has to provide twenty-four-hour written notice.

Walking to the back of the quaint mountain cafe decorated in flashy paintings from recent Open Canvas Nights and local artists, I recognize the Rough & Ready Romance Readers Club, filled with the people who have become my closest pals since moving here. Oddly enough, they include more than one of Rock's sisters-in-law. With fourteen foster brothers in a town of two thousand, trying to avoid these familial ties is impossible.

As for the man himself, it sounds like he's on the road a lot, touring with his rockabilly band, the Lowlifes, so there's no risk of accidentally bumping into him, though he owns the town's one tattoo parlor, Wicked Skin.

Even there, he's never around, relying on guys like Muffin and Coolie to run the place and dole out the permanent artwork. I don't know what either man's real name is, but both do good work, although Coolie definitely has the lighter hand.

I've learned this by stopping in a couple times for fun little tattoos, including swallows and roses on my upper right arm and a Sailor Jerry-style cowgirl on the inside of my left wrist. I wasn't sure how conservative this town would be and whether parents would be down with my vintage ink. But the kids love it, and the parents don't seem to mind. Honestly, I get a lot of compliments on the work.

Delilah, the redheaded owner of The Human Being, greets me, wrapping me in a firm embrace. She's covered in extravagant ethnic jewelry and a flowing dress that would give my hippie grandmother a run for her money. Dee's got a thing going with Rock's brother, Holden, but he's in prison, although I've never poked around to find out why.

Jess rounds the table to greet me, moving slowly, thanks to her adorable baby bump that appears to be growing by the day. The perky blonde with a chic bob is a true crime reporter who's always dressed to the nines, even nearly eight months pregnant. She's married to Logan, another of Rock's brothers.

Logan's a burly, dark-haired, bearded search and rescue guy, a fact that reassures me every time I go hiking in the area. Thanks to my arrival in October after the previous kindergarten teacher left for unexpected back surgery, I've only gotten to do a little outdoor exploring, but I have big hopes for this next spring and summer.

Alex has piercing crystal blue eyes and a mane of thick, glossy black curls. She's a classical cellist and accompanies me for Mommy and Me singalongs on Saturday mornings at this location. She and her husband, Maksim, a towering, surly blond mountain man, have the most adorable toddler, Dmitri, and both have attended each event so far.

It's a new thing I started about a month ago, and Delilah swears up and down that it's increased her business. Personally, I enjoy the chance to mingle with people and feel more connected to the community. As an added bonus, many of my kindergartners and their parents come, enhancing the bond with my students and their families. Without these events to look forward to, I wouldn't have stuck out this move so far.

I mean, Hollister has no drive-thru Starbucks, no vast malls filled with posh stores and unnecessary products, no massive mega-seller bookstores. No health food stores chock full of organic produce and overpriced supplements.

Heck, there's only one restaurant, the Silver Fork, although the food is delectable, and the head chef and owner, Jerry, who looks more like a linebacker than a cook, is a real kick. Originally from NYC, he represents a big-city lifeline to me, as do Delilah, Jess, and Alex—all from the Bay Area. They give me hope that someday, I'll quit thinking about all the things I miss about Sac. I have my doubts, though.

Rounding out the crew is Roxy with her glossy black braids and kind, round face. She rushes towards me, folding me enthusiastically in her arms. "How are you, Chica?" I don't know why, but that's what she calls me. "We missed you at the shelter the other day. I swear Mr. Moody curses more when you're not volunteering."

I chuckle. Mr. Moody's an African grey parrot who showed up a couple of weeks ago because his elderly owner died. Somehow, the crotchety old feathered fellow and I hit it right off. He's gorgeous and mouthy with a sarcastic sense of humor and enough advanced age to ensure he never flies away from me.

"Well, I'm not a huge fan of driving in the snow, even with chains. So, my foul-mouthed, plumed soulmate will just have to be patient."

She laughs.

I hold up the book in my gloved hand, looking around the table and exclaiming, "This book! Oh my God!" I don't know what else to say.

Everyone laughs.

"Give me a hot, brooding, tattooed, bad-boy cowboy any day!" *Did I say I don't do bad boys? Only in real life. But in fiction, they're free game.*

Dee's eyebrows shoot up, and her cheeks darken. I'd give a whole quarter for her thoughts, although I'm guessing they're somewhat mischievous by the expression on her face. She observes, "Brody's pretty damn tough to beat."

I nod, removing my coat and gloves and taking a seat. I look around the table at the delectable caffeinated drinks in quirky mugs and extra-large teacups served on saucers. Some, like Jess's decaf cappuccino, have artsy hearts and leaves in the foam, Dee's barista trademark.

"What can I get you?" the redhead asks, standing up and filling the air with the sounds of her clanging accessories and patchouli oil-based fragrance.

"You know," I say with a teasing lilt.

"A peppermint hot chocolate with extra candy cane bits sprinkled over the whipped cream on top."

"You are the best, Dee!" The other readers around the table nod in agreement. I may generally go for a super healthy lifestyle. Mushroom coffee in the morning, green tea throughout the day, mostly vegan food, and daily exercise, whether it's a quick morning run or some evening yoga. But I wholeheartedly, one hundred percent believe in the occasional hedonistic splurge. Otherwise, how's life worth living?

Jess sits back, absent-mindedly, rubbing her belly, which protrudes more since our last book club meeting a week ago. "When Lyla noticed the bear tattoo on his ribs and then researched and figured out who Brody's father was. Oh my gosh, I balled like a baby."

"No offense," Alex chimes in, "But pregnancy may have had a little something to do with that."

"What? Are you seriously telling me you didn't cry during the big reveal?"

Alex shrugs. "I teared up a little bit. But balled like a baby? No, I'm chalking that up as a third-trimester thing."

"I didn't cry at all," I chuckle. "I was too busy anticipating that scorching sex scene when they finally admitted their pasts to each other and got so vulnerable. I mean, Brody may have looked and acted like a total loser player on the surface. But damn, once he claimed Lyla, he was so soft and melty...only for her. Why can't real men be like that?" My voice fades out, dreamy and soft.

"They are," Roxy pipes in with a mischievous smile. I've had this conversation with these ladies before.

"I mean, men that aren't already taken."

"Good luck with that," Jess says with a smirk. "Honestly, Logan was a total player when I met him. Some of the pickup lines that came out of his mouth. But he was worth ignoring every one of them. And I was no picnic to date, either. I had a strict no-relationship rule."

Alex bursts into giggles, nodding at her best friend's stomach. "Can we all agree you kind of messed that up?"

The blonde laughs, nodding. "Yeah, I guess you could say being nearly eight months pregnant is a no-strings-attached, one-night-stand done spectacularly wrong. But I couldn't be happier with my mountain-man bad boy."

"Hmm..." I think out loud. "I've never thought about bad boys working out in real life. I mean, my father was such a loser. Totally a deadbeat...you know. Even more ill-equipped to be a parent than my mom, which is saying something."

All eyes turn towards me, and I shift in my seat uncomfortably. *Thank you again, unfiltered mouth.*

Chapter Two

EFFIE

Roxy asks softly, "When did you last see your father?"

"Like never," I shrug. "Everything I know about him, I learned from my mom. And as you've no doubt already figured out, she had nothing nice to say."

"Have you ever tried to reach out to him? Get his side of the story?" Dee asks, carefully setting the red and white decorated hot cocoa in a lovely vintage cup and saucer in front of me. Leave it to Dee. Always trying to give people the benefit of the doubt.

"No, although he wouldn't be hard to contact, seeing as Scared and Dazed still tours and everything. My dad's the lead singer of that band. I don't know. Seems like a Pandora's Box to me."

In truth, and I won't admit this to anyone, I fear his final, painful, complete rejection of me. Even though I don't know the man at all, something about the specter of it puts a frisson of dread down my spine. Some things are better left unknown and unfinished.

"Your dad is Sax Gunner?" Dee asks, arching a thin, scarlet eyebrow.

"Yes," I sigh, studying the peppermint bits on the top of my whipped cream more closely than I need to. "And he abandoned my mom and me without a call, letter, email, signed fucking photograph. Nothing. Nada. Like my existence wasn't even worth his acknowledgment."

The table settles into an uneasy silence. Dee's face looks conflicted, as if she's trying to work something out in her head. I kick myself internally for oversharing, but the subject of bad-boy rockers brings out vitriol in me.

Finally, Jess weighs in. "It might be nice, with the holidays and all, to reach out to him. Although I know better than anyone how disastrously that can turn out. After I first found out I was pregnant with Oliver, I called my parents in San Francisco only to learn they're still functioning alcoholics. They drink more than ever. Have no interest in me and my life. And, yeah, I don't want them in my child's life in any shape or form."

Alex noticeably winces next to her.

Jess's eyes narrow, looking at her. "What?"

Alex frowns. "It's sad. That's all. I mean, they always seemed like nice people when I saw them. But I know what you told me over the years and why you had to emancipate early."

"That's why they're called functioning alcoholics. Emancipating at sixteen was one of the best decisions of my life," the blonde says, quirking her mouth. "Logan and I both come from horrible home situations and sometimes it scares me thinking about this whole parenting thing with no healthy blueprint apart from Logan's foster upbringing. But I'm hell-bent on doing better for Oliver."

"You and Logan will do great. I don't have a doubt in my mind," Alex replies reassuringly.

"One hundred percent agreed," Roxy chimes in with one of her infectious smiles, her cheeks rosy and radiant.

"Families!" I exclaim, not wanting to dive any deeper into that mire. "Enough about all of that drama. What are you guys doing for Christmas?"

I listen distractedly as one woman at a time answers, going around the table, my thoughts still half-focused on my father. I try to push the possibility of contacting him from my mind. After all, I don't need two parents to take care of.

The women speak of a big Christmas Eve party at Rough & Ready Ranch, everyone of them inviting me in turn, although I politely refuse. If ever there was a spot where I might see my Lazarus, this would be it. It's seriously the last thing I need right now. His first impression was more than strong enough to be his last.

"No, I'm heading over the hill to spend the week with Mom. We've got it all planned out. A Boxing Day shopping spree filled with malls, restaurants, all the big-city stuff I've been missing." I grin from ear to ear, all the happiness of the holiday season pinned on this mini escape.

"Sounds fantastic," says Roxy, sitting back, her eyes fixating on the wall as she daydreams.

"You better watch the weather," Jess warns. "Good luck getting over the pass when it blows in."

My throat tightens at her warning. All I need is Hollister keeping me tightly locked in its clutches with blizzard-related drama. I don't know what I'll do if I get stuck here this holiday season. Thankfully, as a teacher, I'm on vacation and can skip out early if need be. I make a mental note to call Mom later to firm up our plans.

"Alright, enough about the holidays. Let's talk Brody and Lyla... That barn scene. Oh. My. God," I say, eliciting smiles and darkened cheeks from the rest of the romance readers.

The hour passes so quickly that I have to look twice at the

clock. As we head to the cafe's doors, hugging and wishing each other a safe drive home, Dee catches my eye. "Will we be seeing you for Mommy and Me tomorrow morning?"

I nod enthusiastically.

Her eyes tick towards Alex, and the raven-haired curvy girl nods firmly. "I'll be there, too, and so will Maksim and Dmitri."

"I think Logan and I will, too," Jess chimes in with a smile. "I'm easing him into listening to kids' music."

"Well, this is a fantastic way to do it," Dee says, making my heart swell with pride. "If Holden and I had children, they'd listen to a steady diet of Effie, Lynyrd Skynyrd, the Grateful Dead, and Pfish."

Roxy agrees with a chuckle. "I love your music and songs, Effie, and I don't even have kids. Although fingers crossed, Hawk and I are working on it."

The revelation hits me that soon every woman I know in this town will be married with children except for Dee and me. And Dee has an excuse with her man in prison. *What's mine?* All I know is I don't want to think about it tonight.

On the drive back to my place, I get Mom on speaker-phone as I crunch tentatively along the slick, ice-covered roads to my house.

"Babe, what are you up to?" she answers breathlessly.

"Is this a bad time?" I ask, hearing a man's deep voice in the background. It wouldn't be the first time I caught Mom in the middle of the horizontal mambo with one of her loser boyfriends.

"It's as good as any time. I've been meaning to call you. Just been super, super busy."

I clearly make out a "Who is it?" in grumbly registers.

Although my mom tries to whisper, I hear her answer, "Nobody."

I sigh. Wouldn't be the first time she's hidden the fact she has a kid from one of her new beaus. She has to, considering how liberally she undercounts her age. *Whatever*.

I had hoped over the years, she'd outgrow some of her immaturity. But some things never change. I thought the sting of her answer would also fade with time... Maybe I'm overly sensitive.

I say, "I just wanted to firm up our holiday plans. Things are getting pretty rough here weather-wise, so I'm thinking about heading your way tomorrow or the day after."

Silence.

"You know, before the pass closes, and I get stuck here." I try hard to keep my voice steady, but it trembles slightly at the end. I scold myself internally for being such a baby.

"About that..."

Here it comes...

"I hope you won't be terribly disappointed. But I'm going to need to take a rain check on our holiday plans. Work's been really tough these past couple of weeks. And I just can't make the time right now. I hope you understand?"

She doesn't care if I understand. Anger flashes inside me, hot as a skillet slick with boiling oil. Why did I honestly think things would be different this year? Because sometimes they are. Usually, when Mom's sad and lonely post-breakup, and she needs someone to comfort her. Most of the time, however, things remain predictably stupid like this. Maybe the real question is why I never learn?

"I understand," I say softly, in a voice that sounds hollowed out. *I'm not nearly as interesting as whichever Tom, Dick, or Harry you've glommed onto this holiday season. Just fucking blood of your blood. That's all.* But instead of voicing these thoughts, I bite my bottom lip hard, trying not to sob.

My mother's laughter mixes with a male's chuckles in the distance, and she exclaims, "Oh!" I can only guess what's going on. "Look, I'll give you a call on Christmas, okay?

Hang in there and enjoy your first small-town holiday celebration!"

Tears flood my eyes as I end the call on my Volvo's Bluetooth device. The rich, dark tones of Michael Bublé belting out Christmas carols seize the car's interior. I shut it off vindictively, turning all my rage on the knob of my radio. It deserves better, but shit rolls downhill.

Hot streams roll over my cold cheeks, and I sob, feeling like the lonely little girl my mother neglected every time a shiny, new boy toy came along. Some things never change.

Tears blind my eyes, and I have to pull over, resting my head on the steering wheel and sobbing. Mom's done this too many times to count, so why does it hurt so much this year? Maybe because, despite the happy face I put on for everyone, I'm lonely. Utterly, entirely, one-hundred percent lonely with no hope of remedying the situation.

Until a thought hits me. It's no long-term solution, but it could help get me through the holidays alone. Tomorrow, I'll call Roxy about fostering a new pet over the holidays. And I'm going to hit up Muffin and Coolie for a new tattoo. Maybe a parrot to commemorate Mr. Moody, the closest I'll ever get to a soulmate. Or some roses on my calf.

If I don't stay busy and push through this holiday season alone, I know myself. I'll get so mired and bogged down in the whole thing it'll take all of January to dig back out of depression. My kindergartners deserve better than that. With the feelings welling up inside, though, it may be inevitable. But I still have to try.

Chapter Three

ROCK

"What in the fuck?" I growl into my phone line, unable to ignore the ringing any longer. Only family and very close friends call me at this number. And to successfully reach me, they also have to know I'm home. All of this means they also know I absolutely fucking hate mornings, so to say I'm pissed is an understatement. My bleary eyes make out seven-thirty on Saturday morning. Hell, no.

"Is this how you deal with telemarketers these days?" a cheery female voice asks, annoying me even more. Delilah. The sweet, Bohemian redhead is one of the few people on the planet I can't get mad at, even though she knows better than to call at this time.

"Baby girl, you know it's too fucking early for this shit. Let me give you a call back—"

"Don't hang up. Or I'll keep calling."

"Fuck, Dee. Somebody better be dead."

"That's real nice," she says with a slight tremor in her voice. I've always had a dark sense of humor, and normally, she gets this. But she's also become more sensitive over the years, what with my brother, Holden, in prison. She's confided in me before that her biggest fear is a phone call with bad news about him behind bars. It's already happened once, although, fortunately, he survived. Anyway, I should know better than to say things like this to her. But dammit, it's not even eight yet!

"Sorry. But you know how I am in the morning. Fuck, girl, promise me you won't make this a habit."

"I won't," she replies with a chuckle.

"Once upon a time, if memory serves me right, you weren't too keen on early mornings either. Until the caffeine business started messing with your internal clock."

"No, I figured out how much I was missing out on before rising at noon. You have to realize I make the bulk of my money before nine."

Pressing my phone's speaker button, I roll over, scrubbing my eyes with the heels of my hands. "Yeah, well, as a musician and tattoo artist, I make most of mine after nine, and I don't mean in the morning. So, can you explain why you've woken me? I was having the best dream about Pamela Anderson from her *Baywatch Days*..."

I detect a moment's hesitation before Dee says, "I'm cleaning out my office and getting ready for a new year and new me. You know all of that, and I'm tired of holding onto your acoustic guitar. Are you coming down here to get it, or am I pawning it?"

I sit up stock straight in bed, shaking the sleep from my head. "No, Dee. Absolutely not. That's signed by Brian Setzer with the hand-drawn dice sketch. What the fuck are you even thinking right now?"

"If it's worth so much, maybe you should come get it. And could you lay off the colorful language with me? Don't you know how to talk to a lady?" she teases, although her voice betrays a testy edge.

"I've never had any problem with the ladies, but we don't do a lot of talking," I laugh mischievously.

"Well, I guess everybody has to be good at something," she says, the sarcasm dripping from her voice. "Anyway, Phil from the Ophir City Pawn Shop will be here around nine to look at a few things I'm ditching, so if you want to keep your baby, you'd better think about getting down here."

"What in the world's gotten into you, girl?" I rasp, frustrated.

"Like I said, new year, new me."

I grumble, scratching my chest, "I want the old Dee back."

"I'd be more worried about getting your instrument back," she replies sassily.

"I cannot believe you right now."

"And I cannot believe how long you've stashed your guitar in my office. You swore you would pick it up in October before leaving on your last tour."

"Yeah, I know. But that was a tough time for me. You know, when I caught Lexie and Bub making out after the show at Stonie's. And then the fistfight and bender and ending up in my cute-as-a-button renter's bushes. You've got to keep me away from that curvy little number, Dee, because she's the kinda girl I could really get into."

Bub's the drummer in my band, and Lexie was my girlfriend of five months. Sure, I always sensed she wasn't the most loyal, but it took seeing her tongue down Bub's throat for me to get the full picture. Which resulted in a drinking bout the likes never seen before or since and a fistfight with Bub that's still simmering drama beneath the surface of the Lowlifes. It probably doesn't help the night was so rough that I've been sober ever since and plan on keeping it that way.

Funny story or not, waking up pinned to a thorn bush to the sound of an angel singing was akin to a near-death experience for me. As in, I saw the fucking light real fast and refuse to go back to my most miscreant ways.

Fortunately, sobriety hasn't been tough as many of my friends are already straight-edge, including Muffin and Coolie. But going sober and doing the whole Alcoholics Anonymous thing has only exacerbated things with the rest of the Lowlifes, who can never say no to shots onstage and sloppy, post-show drinking bashes—not nearly as fun without booze.

She chuckles. "Yes, because nothing worse could happen to you in this life than finding a girl who actually treats you right." Dee was never a fan of Lexie's.

I stretch, yawning loudly as I drape my legs over the side of the bed, plopping my big naked feet on the cold wood floor of my cabin. I still need to get a damn rug in here. "You and I both know I'd destroy that angel. I'm a walking, fucking disaster. And this whole mess with Lexie and Bub remains next level, not something I want to drag anyone else into."

"How do you mean?"

"Lexie's trying to play Bub and me against each other. There's always some new drama or problem to deal with, and honestly, I am so over it."

"That's frustrating. I hate to say this, but she always struck me as a narcissist."

I run my hand through my hair, reflecting on the last five months of my life. "That would explain a lot. I just want all of this over with. You know what I mean?"

"As in the Lowlifes over with? Or not seeing Lexie anymore?"

"All of the above."

"Well, don't do anything rash," she warns.

"Oh, I won't. But I'd like an out. As fun as it's been, I think the Lowlifes have run their course."

"On the bright side, it was a good run."

"Yeah..."

"And on another bright side, I promise to have your fave drink waiting for you when you arrive. One large white chocolate mocha with extra whipped cream."

"It sounds so fucking—sorry, so frou-frou when you say it like that. My secret girlie drink remains top secret. Just between you and me."

"Of course, Landry. Now, get your butt down here before Phil makes off with your strings."

Dee likes to use my last name, and I wonder if it's her way of keeping me at arm's length. Not that I'd ever infringe on Holden's territory, but I'm naturally flirty.

"You better not let that happen." A warning growl wells up deep within my chest, resonant and dangerous.

"Are you seriously growling? Keep that up, and I'm going to get you a rabies shot. Geez."

Delilah's seriously the only woman who knows how to handle me. That's why I love busting her chops. But she and I both know she only has eyes for my brother. Lucky bastard.

"Can you throw a couple of extra shots in my drink? I'm going to need them after your rude awakening."

"Espresso shots, right?"

I laugh. But I have to admit her question's valid. Not so long ago, when I fully embraced the rockstar lifestyle, the type of shots might have been anybody's guess. "Yes, espresso. I told you. I've turned over a new leaf. I'm going all Sting and shit with healthy eating, yoga, and sobriety."

"Just making sure. See you soon, Rocker."

An hour later, I come through the back door of The Human Being, where delivery trucks drop off supplies. It's not like I'm famous and have to avoid crowds or anything. Honestly, the Lowlifes is for a very specific core of diehard rockabilly and psychobilly fans. But people in town recognize my face and enjoy chatting for inordinate lengths of time. I might be able to begrudgingly handle this socializing this afternoon, but not before nine.

I knock on Dee's door, admiring her copies of vintage psychedelic rock posters, only to be met with a deafening silence. As I wait in front of her door, I hear guitar strumming and power chords. As I spy down the long hallway into the cafe, I see people gathered with lots of kids. Following the sounds, I'm drawn like a sailor to a siren, ensnared by the most angelic voice I've ever heard. One that hits me with its familiarity, like a dream I've had before.

Standing at the back of the cafe, I scrutinize the stage where a diminutive, curvy woman in tight-fitting dark-wash Levi's folded at the bottom, black and white Van's, and a black cardigan with a Johnny Cash T-shirt underneath sits on a high stool with a guitar, singing into a microphone on a stand. Josephine Jackson. Next to her, Alex sits with her cello, playing a sinewy, robust accompaniment as children cheer and dance around like they know what's coming next.

From her red lipstick to her short, scarlet-tipped nails and curly Marilyn Monroe-style ebony hair tied up with a black and white bandana, she's the black cat I need in my life. A rocker chic dreamboat, the likes of which I never see around Hollister. Sexy, edgy, vintage, and talented AF.

Except she's the epitome of off-limits...too young, innocent, and drama-free (as far as I can tell) to drag into my complicated existence. Oh, and she's the unruly tenant I should find the balls to evict. There's that, too. Yet, I eye her with an uncontainable admiration, swallowing hard.

The woman's voice slides over the lyrics with a pure, haunting, resonant quality and luscious vibrato that runs through me like the crystal-clear cascades of an alpine stream. Refreshing, pristine, and tinged with those otherworldly qualities I remember from the morning I woke up under a bush.

My breath catches in my throat, taking her in, and, my

cock strains against my zipper. So much for self-control. Her large, expressive, lavender eyes, heart-shaped face, and full, cherry-stung lips present an intoxicating visual as her melody floats around the room, enveloping me in its exotic, feminine beauty.

I try to breathe, unable to move. Pinned to the sounds emanating from the lovely woman, so unadulterated they could cut straight through every evil deed I've ever committed and all the havoc I have yet to wreak. Her notes contain a soft, alluring comfort that takes every unnamed demon roiling around inside me and lulls it into quiet peace.

Chapter Four

ROCK

Dee observes, "She has a nice voice, doesn't she?" The redhead comes up beside me, cocking her head in Josephine's direction.

"Didn't I tell you less than an hour ago to keep me away from this minx?" I ask testily.

Dee smiles ambiguously, and her out-of-character call this morning suddenly makes sense. She wanted to lure me here to get a load of this. "Would you believe she's Sax Gunner's daughter?"

I raise an eyebrow, side-eyeing the cafe owner.

"I got it straight from the horse's mouth."

I cock my head to the side, watching my tenant and listening more closely. "She definitely has his pipes."

Dee nods. "Yep, and a lot of pent-up rage because she thinks he abandoned her. Do you know the guy at all?"

I nod, absent-mindedly rubbing the spot over my heart. "Yeah, we've been on some of the bigger tours together. He comes across as a super nice family man..."

"Yeah, that's how the media always portrays him, so I'm confused. Makes me wonder what more there is to the story."

I shrug, wondering why Dee tells me any of this.

My eyes flicker back to the stage and the sassy woman singing like the reincarnation of Wanda Jackson. Not only does she have a great voice, but she has a natural presence that catches and keeps an audience's attention. As annoyed as it makes me, I can't help myself, firmly planted under the spell of this divine creature, this raven-haired songstress who has my heart without even asking for it.

Fuck.

The song ends, and the children bounce around, clapping and screaming. They range in age from infants on their mothers' laps to toddlers bustling about and older kids that look like they're school-aged. But I don't know much about kids, so I can't say for sure.

Josephine's eyes tick toward mine, and the air sucks out of the room. Her cheeks flush like bruised rose petals, and she looks down self-consciously, swallowing hard.

"Rock!" Alex screams across the cafe, waving with her hand. "Come up and jam with us."

"Oh, h—" I catch myself before cursing in front of a roomful of minors. "No, I couldn't possibly."

Dee turns to me with a knowing smile, handing me the case with the acoustic guitar signed by Brian Setzer. "Your drink's on the house if you serenade us, along with endless refills."

I frown, grimacing. "I don't know any kid-friendly songs," I hiss.

"Come on up, Bro. Just a song or two," Alex's sunshiny voice rises over the room's din. Goddammit!

As I make my way towards the front, I scope out Maksim holding Dmitri and Logan and Jess seated near the front, with broad smiles on their faces. I swear Jess looks twice as pregnant since last I saw her.

Dee comes up behind me with a second tall stool, and the

fix is in. Side-eyeing my tenant, her face remains flushed, indicating she's not in on any of this. Thank goodness.

But I can't tell if her bright cheeks stem from embarrassment, anger, or something else. When her eyes settle on my face, her lips pressed into a tight line, I decide on rage. I can't blame her. After all, I'm stealing her stage.

"Nice to see you again, renter," I grunt, setting the guitar case on a table behind us and pulling out the black acoustic number. I tune as I talk, "You keeping the place feline-free these days?"

She shrugs, looking down guiltily. Despite the wholesome appearance, this one's trouble—from her rocker outfit to her firebrand of a mouth, her obvious dislike of authority and rules to the Sailor Jerry cowgirl I glimpse on the ivory skin on the underside of her left wrist. It looks new enough to be the work of Muffin or Coolie. Apparently, I've missed out on a lot while touring.

"I'll make this quick," I promise with a wink, launching into the opening chords of "Between the Bars" by Elliott Smith and perching on the stool next to the delectable woman. Leaning forward into the mic, I launch into the first verse, enjoying the sounds of the acoustic guitar and the way it fills the room. A kid-friendly song? Not so much. But it's about as innocent as it gets in my repertoire.

My voice hovers over the brooding lyrics, exploiting a tenor range I rarely enter as a rockabilly artist. Women around the room cock their heads to the side, leaning back and relaxing into the lyrics. Some of them relax their lips, dropping open slightly in that inviting way groupies look at me on the road. And the men in the room, including my brothers, cross their arms, sitting straighter, aware of the seduction simmering beneath the surface, even though I try my best to keep things on the up and up.

Alex joins in with sultry cello notes, filling the room with an ethereal ambiance in stark contrast to my normal shows. The lyrics tangle around me, spilling into the room with a bittersweet allure until something so magical and unexpected happens that I almost stop singing.

Josephine leans into the mic next to me.

There's no way she knows these words. She's way too young for this song...

But to my astonishment, her sensual voice accompanies mine, like the glittering essence of champagne, shimmering just above my own, her hand lightly tapping time on her guitar. She doesn't try to out-sing me or take the lead in the song. Instead, her heavenly voice dances and flirts with mine, adding a purity and dimension I didn't know my vocals needed.

The vulnerability of the moment, our faces inches apart, our breaths co-mingling as we concentrate on weaving our voices around each other's, feels akin to musical lovemaking, only in front of a roomful of people. My heart pounds chaotically in my chest. Alex's cello lines snake around our vocals, tying them together in a strange perfection that leaves all three of us breathless and motionless after the final chorus.

"Wow," I manage, glancing at my singing partner. She blinks hard as though stunned, and I can tell by the quizzical expression on her face she feels it, too. Whatever this is.

Raucous applause breaks out in the cafe, surprising me even more as I look out at the audience. Jess wipes tears from her eyes, as do a handful of other women, and Dee looks shocked.

"Thank you," I say, nodding towards Josephine and Alex and standing up.

Dee rushes to the front of the stage. "Don't stop now. Do another one. Or do that one again. Please, that was...I don't know how to describe it. But yeah, please. One more."

"Nah," I say, shaking my head and shooting a furtive look

towards Josephine. "This is her concert, not mine. I don't want to steal the attention."

The curvy angel swallows hard, "It's okay." But her face looks too stony to read.

"Yeah?" I ask. I look up for a moment, my head brainstorming ideas. I search for something a little indie and alternative, where we can continue exploring whatever our voices just did together. "'Sour Times' by Portishead?" I'll be surprised if the twenty-something knows this one.

To my amazement, she smiles broadly, nodding her head.

I say, "You'll have to take the lead. You good with that?"

"Of course," she replies, raising her chin defiantly and shooting me a look that steals my breath and my heart. I've really got to watch it with this girl.

The concert goes on, one eclectic cover after another: The Romantik's "Talking in Your Sleep," Michael Jackson's "Billie Jean," The Smashing Pumpkins' "Slow Dawn," The Goo Goo Dolls' "Black Balloon."

Five songs in, and the audience is begging for a return appearance. The singing range and musical knowledge of my tenant astound me. A couple of times, one or the other of us falters on a lyric or two, but the overall impression glosses over these minor mistakes. If we can make music like this unrehearsed, what could we do with some practice? Side-eyeing my singing partner and sister-in-law, Alex, I smile a little embarrassed and a lot surprised.

I shrug. "A return appearance? It's up to you two," I propose, nodding toward Alex and Josephine. I gave up performing for free a long time ago. But for this experience? Hell, yeah, I'd do it again in a heartbeat.

Alex laughs, "Whenever I can break away from Maksim and Dmitri, I'd love to do this again."

But my singing partner grimaces, trying to look at me without making eye contact, that same unreadable expression on her face. "It was fun. But I don't know. I think I'd rather stick to what I'm already doing." The pained smile on her face communicates something else.

Women don't say "no" to me often, but I still know how to take a hint. Standing up, I show my palms to the audience, still clutching the guitar in one hand. "Sorry, folks. That was a one-time deal. But thanks for listening." Turning back towards the stage, I hug Alex. "Good to see you again, Sis." When I approach Josephine for a hug, she's casing her guitar, her face downright sour. "Nice seeing you again, Josephine."

"I go by Effie," she says, a cold edge to her voice.

"Sorry, Effie. Good seeing you again. Thanks for letting me share the stage with you for a bit."

"About that…" she says, finally looking at me. Her cheeks go from warm to hot, the electricity sizzling between our gazes undeniable.

"Yeah?" My heart thumps against my ribs, hoping she's changed her mind about doing this whole duet thing. I need to perform with her again, try to figure out this strange, alchemical reaction going on between us. Sort out why she makes me feel so much and what this jumble of emotions ultimately means.

"It was fun," she concludes, stilted, shifting back when I go for a hug. Instead, I offer her a handshake, but she refuses. Turning back to her guitar, she continues casing up, exuding a level of dislike that even my bush-sleeping antics don't deserve. *What the fuck's up with this woman, and why do I care so much?*

Chapter Five

S tudents and their families line up to talk to me as they have after every show. But I can't be in the same room with Rock for one second longer.

Anger seethes beneath the surface. Anger at him for taking the bait and taking over my show. Anger at him for having the most beautiful male voice I've ever heard. The kind of voice that wraps around mine in undeniable, perfect ways. Like two halves of the same coin. Anger at his swaggering, overly confident attitude, searing turquoise eyes, rippling inked musculature, and rocker, bad-boy persona. Anger at the overwhelming chemistry shuttling back and forth between us that makes me want to jump his bones despite knowing better.

Closing the case and fastening the buckles, I dart for the door. I can't do this with this man.

"Wait," he calls after me. "Let me at least walk you out."

Walk me out? Do I look like I need a man to walk me anywhere? Last time I checked, I live in a town of two thousand people. What's his escort outside going to protect me from? Myself?

"I'm good. Bye," I call coldly over my shoulder, putting

my head down and rushing through the crowd of concert attendees with a thin smile and curt head nods.

Dee's voice calls over the din. "Oh, Rock, don't forget your guitar again!"

"I'll be right back," his deep voice grumbles, and I can hear by its proximity that he follows me.

Great! I head for my white Volvo, picking up the pace, but he cuts me off, launching himself between me and my car before I press the fob to unlock it. Besides singing, his hidden talent seems to be insinuating himself where he doesn't belong.

"Wait, don't go yet," he orders, putting his hands on his hips and catching his breath.

"What?" I frown, every muscle in my body taut and ready to go multiple rounds with him, whether the subject's fostering cats when I shouldn't, bush sleeping, or what happened on stage.

He throws a thumb over his shoulder, pointing towards the cafe. "That was amazing back there. Don't you think?"

I shrug, narrowing my eyes and standing back on my heels to put a little more space between us, even though I'm unwilling to step back and let him think he physically intimidates me.

His eyes widen, and his eyebrows shoot up questioningly. "Effie, I've spent much of my adult life performing, and *that* has never happened to me. In fact, I've waited a lifetime to make music like that." He furrows his brows as if saying again *don't you agree?*

"It was okay. People seemed to like it—"

"People were fucking crying in the audience."

I shake my head, a little puff of air escaping my lips. "No offense, but your sister-in-law, Jess, weeps over everything lately. You know, all those pregnancy hormones."

He shifts his weight, drilling down into me with his eyes.

"So, what happened back there on that stage is normal for you? Common place? You make music like that all the time?"

I open my mouth to protest when a departing family with two kids interrupts us. I recognize them as the Mathers because their son, Landon, is in my kindergarten class. Mrs. Mather exclaims, "That was the most amazing duet I've ever heard. I really hope you two will reconsider performing together again. I mean, it gave me goosebumps."

I paint on a thin smile, and my patience feels unusually thin. "Thank you."

"See?" Rock says, looking at me long and hard, a muscle in his jaw jumping as he grits his teeth together.

"I'm a kindergarten teacher. I have a decent, respectable job and only do music on the weekends because it's fun. But I don't take pay for it, and I don't like sharing the stage with others." I'm lying again because I can't tell Rock the truth.

I refuse to have anything to do with bad-boy rockers, and if I keep seeing you and singing with you, I know I'll break my own rule.

"Oh my goodness! That was amazing!" A familiar voice interrupts. Looking over, I see redheaded Lily with her husband, Turner. The handsome cowboy tips his hat at me. They've got five children from elementary to middle school aged, so I see and speak with her often.

"Thank you," I say politely.

"I didn't see you, Lily, and the kids were here," Rock says, leaning forward to hug each family member. I can't imagine what it must be like to have such a large family and be so close.

"We stayed in the back because Rose and Jack were being especially...precocious today," Turner explains, choosing his words with care. "No offense, Bro, because you know I enjoy the Lowlifes. But this...whatever you two just did onstage was amazing. I'd pay to listen to music like that, and from what I heard people murmuring in the audience, so would they."

Am I in a nightmare or something? Because this is my worst-case scenario ever. Why in the world is this happening to me?

"I agree," the bad boy says, stepping closer to me. His spicy, musky cologne wraps around me. "I'd love to do this again if I can talk this pretty little number into agreeing."

"What?" Lily's eyes widen. "You're not sure about performing with Rock again?"

I shrug. "I make kids music. That's my thing."

"Well, adults deserve good music, too," she laughs.

Now, I've got eight pairs of eyes looking expectantly, the three adults and five kids. *Great. Just great.*

"We'll see what my schedule allows. Things are busy, though, with school and everything."

"I seriously hope you'll reconsider. So when are you leaving to go see your mom for Christmas?" Lily asks, making the backs of my eyes sting. I know it's not her fault. Her question couldn't be more innocent, but it cuts right to the quick of my current vulnerabilities. I kick myself for having mentioned my plans to her in passing. I should've never trusted my mom to stick to one of her promises.

"Sadly, my plans have fallen through. But that's okay," I say, trying to look happy but coming across as decidedly morose. "Because a quiet Christmas at home sounds good to me." I concentrate hard on not sounding like a loser, but a perceptible tremble punctuates my words.

"You can't celebrate alone," the redhead says, instructing Rosie and Jack to hold on as the two mischievous twins hang from her hands, growing impatient. Both attend first grade at the school. "You should come to the Rough & Ready Christmas Eve party. We'd love to have you."

I shrug. "Thank you. But I'm not feeling up to a big celebration now," I excuse, looking down. I leave out the part about this being my fifth rejection of this particular invitation.

The only thing lonelier than spending the holidays without loved ones is spending it with somebody else's loved ones, a close-knit family where you don't belong. Talk about an outsider looking in.

Out of the corner of my eyes, I notice Rock scrutinizing me. Thankfully, he doesn't say anything.

"Well, if you change your mind, you know where to find us. I can't think of anything better than you two performing at the Christmas party. Wouldn't Wyatt love it?" Lily asks Rock and Turner.

"Dad would be all kinds of down for that," Rock answers.

Turner agrees, "Yeah, but you'd have to brush up on your vintage cowboy songs, too. Because he'll bombard you with requests for 'Happy Trails' and stuff like that."

Although I try to keep emotion from my face, curiosity must bleed through as I glance at Lily because she fills in, "Wyatt is Turner and Rock's foster dad and my father-in-law. He's the sweetest old cowboy. But yeah, he would definitely want to hear everything ever sung by Roy Rogers."

Why do I suddenly feel like a calf getting roped in the rodeo ring? All eyes focused on me.

"Lily, I'm hungry," Jack whines.

Rosie joins in. "And I need to go potty!"

Lily's face looks apologetic as she says, "Looks like we're headed back inside the cafe. Anyway, please promise me you'll at least think about it." Her blue eyes pierce me, and all I can do is nod. I feel bad for Turner. I bet that man can never say "no" to her.

As they leave, Rock leans back against my car, crossing his arms and smiling languidly. "You know, it'd mean a lot to me if you'd consider Lily's invitation." He clears his throat. "I mean, our invitation."

I look up at the sky, letting out a long sigh. If my mother hadn't messed everything up with her new boyfriend, I would have an easy out. But instead, I feel dangerously close to falling right into the one trap I promised I would never let myself get snared by. The trap of a charming, charismatic, bad-boy musician. My tongue darts out to lick my lips, and I notice with satisfaction how his turquoise eyes follow it, a sudden yearning crossing his face. It matches what he does to my body whenever we share a room.

"I might even reconsider that no-pet clause," he says, raising an eyebrow.

"You and I both know I'll continue to foster cats either way, and I doubt you have the chutzpah to kick me out."

"Try me," he says, his eyes cold and steely.

"Really? You're going to use vulnerable little kitties to force me to do something I don't want to?"

"If you don't want to, then consider this conversation over," he says, pushing away from the car with a burst of energy that startles me. Putting his head down, he starts back towards the cafe.

"Wait," I call after him, wondering what the hell I'm doing.

He wheels back around, his face dark and clouded. "Look, I don't make anybody do anything against their will. Ever."

"Sorry if that's what I implied. I just... I don't know."

"Don't know what?"

I feel another explosive bout of honesty coming on, even though I try hard to curtail it. "I'm not a huge fan of music and musicians, especially bad-boy, rock-star types."

He stares at me for a long moment, his face twitching as he works out the real meaning behind the words. "Why not? Have you dated one before or something?"

"I'm the offspring of one."

Rock doesn't look surprised as he asks, "Who?"

"It's a long story and not something I want to get into right now. Or ever really." I already said too much yesterday at the romance readers group. The last thing I need is this whole Sax Gunner thing to start circulating as a small-town rumor.

"You know not all rock stars are the same," he ventures, furrowing his brows and looking far too attractive for my sanity. "And besides, you've got a lot more rocker in you than you care to admit. Just look at how you dress and sing."

I'm on the verge of giving in to him and accepting the Christmas invitation. So, instead, I pick a fight. "The problem with all of this is you act like I actually care about your opinion. A guy who whipped out his willy to pee in my bushes the first time we met."

His face goes cold, and his eyes narrow. "No, the problem with all of this is the big fucking chip on your shoulder. Are you trying to tell me you never had a night you weren't proud of or wished you could take back?"

I look down at my toes, unwilling to answer.

"But yeah, if you prefer to act like what happened on stage earlier is nothing, go right ahead. And if you want to spend Christmas alone, that's fine, too. Hell, if you never want to see my face again, I couldn't care less..." He pauses, kicking the dirt in front of him. "Take that last part back. I'm no liar. Nice talking to you as always, Stormy."

"Stormy?"

"Yeah, for a sunshiny, wholesome kindergarten teacher, you've got a bunch of storm clouds lurking just beneath the surface." I open my mouth to reply, but he turns on his heels fast, striding toward The Human Being with an unstoppable purpose.

Stormy. Whatever.

Chapter Six

ROCK

"Hey, Skates, whaddup?" I grumble.

"Rock, you fucking motherfucker, how the fuck are you?"

It still impresses me how many ways Steve "Skates" Harley fits his favorite four-letter word into sentences, and I did seven years in the Navy. "I'm good, man. Merry Christmas."

"Yeah, Merry fucking Christmas to you, too. What can I do you for? I hope you're not calling about the whole deal with Lexie again. As I keep telling Bub, the Lowlifes is a business, and you've got to treat it that way. Put your personal shit aside."

"Nope, Bub can have the bitch. I'm so over that whole situation. I'm actually calling for two reasons."

"Hit me."

"First, I wanted to let you know I'll be sending you some demo tracks after Christmas. Don't expect any fancy recording equipment. Just enough of a listen to give you an idea of a new direction I'm experimenting with. I want your unfiltered take before I go balls deep." *Yeah, right, Rock. Effie doesn't even like being in the same room with you...*

"Alright, can you describe it briefly for me first?"

"Honestly, dude, it's so far out in left field, I couldn't begin to. But I do know it could be highly marketable and a good way to make a quick buck." This is not really how I'd describe the music-making Effie and I did at the cafe, but after years in the biz, I know how to talk to Steve, teasing what interests him most.

"Okay, cool. You've definitely piqued my interest."

"Second, could you put out some feelers and get me in contact with Sax Gunner?"

The line goes silent, although if I strain my ears, I can almost hear the gears in Steve's brain working.

"Sax Gunner? That's random. Wait, does he have something to do with the new project you're sending me?"

"Maybe." I hate speaking opaquely, but I also need to lay the mystique on heavy to ensure Skates sticks to his word and listens to what I send him.

"Aren't Scared and Dazed still with EMZ?" he asks. I hear the fast-paced clicks of a keyboard.

"Not sure..."

"Yeah, let me do a little asking around, and I'll get back to you."

"Thanks, buddy. Happy holidays and don't forget to look for those tracks."

"Sure thing."

After setting my cell phone on my office desk, I stare at the wall of my cabin for a long time, tracing the rough-hewn logs and their shiny golden patina as if a sight never fascinated me more.

What the hell am I doing? Josephine doesn't want anything to do with me, which means she'll likely go ballistic if she finds out I'm reaching out to her long-lost dad. But something about the story she told Dee doesn't make sense. Sax Gunner's one of the nicest, most down-to-earth, most upright singers I know. I can't imagine him being a deadbeat dad. I guess I'll find out soon enough.

All I know is, as a foster kid, hurts from childhood can stick with a person their whole life. Especially if they remain unresolved. Hell, I still go to a therapist to discuss the horror show my neglectful mom and stepdad played out. Chronic lice and hovering in the single-digit percentiles for years finally introduced me to the system. Best thing that ever happened to me.

According to Dee, who I spoke with more when I returned to the cafe to get my guitar after the duets, the Sax Gunner thing is like a gaping hole in Josephine's life. One that still embitters her and makes her disdainful of musicians and singers—bad-boy rockers, as she put it—despite her innate talent. I'd like to help her past some of this like my foster family and therapists helped me. After all, how often will she meet a guy with an in to her estranged father? I feel like I'm meant to do this for her, although I half expect her to kill me for it later.

Of course, I also have ulterior motives, like the fact I can't keep the curvy, dainty minx off my mind or her voice out of my head. It's driving me mad. I wonder how she's doing throughout the day, trying to think up dumbass excuses to show up at her place in my landlord capacity.

I dream about her some nights, a tantalizing mixture of innocent and naughty. And I even find myself doing stupid things like talking about her too much and pumping my sisters-in-law for information. Hell, I've considered "coincidentally" showing up at the next romance readers club or Hollister Elementary—two moves that would land me squarely in stalker territory.

This obvious fixation has earned me some harsh looks from my brothers, who think she's too wholesome and naive for a well-known player like me. Whatever. It's not like I'm some big bad villain with evil intentions.

I'm more like a guy who's a bit transfixed, healthy or otherwise. Besides, it's better than the alternative—ruminating over the fucked up situation with Bub and Lexie, which continues to spiral out of control. I've got to hand it to Lexie for knowing how to keep the pot stirred. She'll be the death of the Lowlifes, but perhaps that's a blessing in disguise. Especially if I can convince Josephine to start singing and recording professionally with me.

Which brings me to my next conclusion. I refuse to let the sunshiny kindergarten teacher spend Christmas Eve alone, even though I know I'm the last person she wants to hang out with. She deserves better, and I'm going to give it to her. Besides, she'll have a blast with my sisters-in-law once she gets over the initial shock. And I can't think of another way to get a recording of our duets to send to Skates. I know the man will love what he hears, and he's gifted and talented when it comes to talking performers into contracts, studio work, and engagements. Fingers crossed, he'll have better luck than me with my stubborn tenant.

Snow pours from the sky in big, weighty flakes that plaster my windshield in white. My wipers squeak and squawk, working overtime. We could all very well get stuck at Rough & Ready Ranch tonight. Should I tell Effie to pack an overnight bag, just in case? I laugh to myself, shaking my head. I'll be lucky to get her to come with me at all, let alone willingly agree to hold up at my childhood home. But I won't let her do the holidays alone. I could tell by the quiver in her voice and the look on her face in the cafe parking lot that the specter of this disturbed her, although she tried hard to play the stoic.

Pulling into the driveway, I hop out, rounding the front of my 1978 dark gray Ford Bronco and marveling at the accumulation on the ground, already fast approaching the tops of my

Doc Martens. Before I reach the door to knock, I notice the blinds by the front door window peel back for a moment, and panicked lavender eyes dart in my direction.

Rapping lightly on the door, I holler through the wood, "It's okay if you have kittens in there. I'm not here to bust you or anything."

I hear rustling on the other side of the door, and footsteps hammering up and down the hallway. Perhaps I caught her in a state of undress? This thought puts a big smile on my face. Now, that's a Christmas present I wouldn't mind receiving. The chain on the door and the click of the lock make my heart pound in double-time as she hesitantly opens it a couple of inches, staring at me. "What?"

"I know manners are different in big cities, but most people greet each other with 'Merry Christmas' or at a bare minimum, 'Happy Holidays' this time of year."

"Merry Christmas." She scowls, wresting a dark chuckle from me. One thing Effie can't do is hide her feelings, something I love about her.

Chapter Seven

ROCK

"**M**ay I come in?" I ask, cocking my head to look past her. She keeps the crack in the door so thin I can't see much.

"According to the law, you must provide written permission twenty-four hours before entering a tenant's home."

"Smart girl," I compliment, leaning forward and putting my hand on the door, pushing it open ever so slightly until my hand meets her arm's resistance. "I promise I won't bite or anything." Clearly another lie, but she doesn't need to know this...yet.

She steps back a little, her mouth falling open in an "O" shape I long to fill with everything from my fingers to my toes and my cock. God, I'm a deviant sometimes. Enough of a deviant to not know better. Instead, I open the door a bit further.

She swallows hard, her eyes rounding. "Is there something you don't understand about 'written' and 'twenty-four hours?'"

"Oh, I'm not here as your landlord. Like I said, I won't even freak out if you have kittens running around like last time, although, for the record, I'm allergic to them—"

"Allergic?" Guilt floods her face. "I'm sorry. I had no idea."

"Yeah," I nod, easing the door open a little more as her arm relaxes and her face transforms from guarded to empathetic. "Something about their fur, dander, or claws makes me break out in little red hives. It's not pretty. But it's also nothing Calamine lotion won't handle, so maybe you should start stocking some if you don't have it already."

"Stocking Calamine? Why would I do that? I'm not allergic to them."

"Because if you persist on keeping things I'm allergic to, it's the least you can do. Don't you think?"

She shakes her adorable, raven-haired head, worrying her luscious cherry-stung bottom lip. It takes every ounce of willpower not to lean forward and suck it into my mouth. I wonder if she tastes as delectable as she looks in tight-fitting, dark-wash skinny jeans, a pale pink cashmere cardigan with a Hello Kitty shirt underneath, and matching striped socks on her tiny feet. "No, because I barely ever see you."

I take a deep breath, feeling more nervous than I should. It's a testament to how much I like this pretty, curvy teacher. "I'd like that to change." I raise an eyebrow.

She frowns. "I don't know."

"You do know. Even if you won't admit it."

"Admit what?" she hisses.

"That at a bare minimum, our voices go together..." I stare at her long and hard, forcing her to reflect before answering instead of stinging me with more careless words from her firebrand mouth. Between music and tattooing, I may not be the kind of guy who has to work hard for pussy, but I've got feelings, too. Pretty damn sensitive ones.

"You're not going to let this go. Are you?"

"Nope," I say, shaking my head firmly and biting my

tongue as a small ball of fur skitters past my boots, followed by another. "How many this time, Stormy?"

She looks like the cat who's swallowed the canary. Shrugging and scrunching her forehead, she whispers, "Three kittens, but no mom."

"Your lack of respect for authority is impressive. I kind of dig it."

"Well," she replies. "It doesn't really matter what you dig, does it?"

I take a step closer to her, and her cheeks flush. Her eyes flood with pure liquid lust, and I chuckle, pleased by my little experiment. "You can pretend it doesn't if you like. But it won't change anything. Now, enough of the pleasantries. I'm not leaving you here alone on Christmas Eve. I know you might feel intimidated at the thought of hanging out with some people you barely know, but there's no more welcoming crew on the planet. Believe me, by the end of the evening, you'll feel like you're a part of the family."

"Oh, I don't know about that..." There's a slight lisp to her words.

"Stormy, that's why I'm not asking you. I'm telling you. Besides, look at this fucking place. Could it get any more depressing? No Christmas tree. No lights. No decorations."

"I've spent many Christmases alone. It's no big deal. She raises a finger, adding, "And I have egg nog." That explains the lisp.

I tuck her first statement in the back of my mind to revisit later. How could someone so young have spent many Christmases alone? "That confirms it. I am not letting you sit here alone, imbibing egg nog all by yourself, drunk and depressed."

She buries her head in her hand, shaking it. "And I'm not going to your family's Christmas Eve gathering buzzed."

"Where's your coffee pot?"

"Coffee pot? Why?"

"Because, in my opinion, there are two optimal ways to sober up. The first is black coffee. So, it's time to caffeinate your pretty little ass."

She laughs, not drunk, but buzzed enough to be more forthright with her facial expressions and comments than usual. "There's nothing pretty or little about my ass."

"You're only half right," I say, stepping closer to her so that she has to crane her head to look up at me. "It's actually pretty and round, with the kind of padding a guy like me would enjoy holding onto. But I assumed you wouldn't appreciate the extra information, so I settled for a figure of speech. Maybe I was wrong?"

Her cheeks flush pink, and she cocks her head to the side. "And what's the second?"

"The second?" I'm so caught up eye-fucking my tenant I can't keep a stray thought in my head. What the hell is my problem?

"Yes, the second way to sober up?" she whispers as breathy as Marilyn Monroe. My cock strains against the zipper of my pants, ready to devour this voluptuous beauty whole.

I growl, "Hot, messy sex."

"Oh!" Her eyes bulge, and her face goes burgundy, although she doesn't step back or betray disinterest. Instead, she looks as embarrassed as a high school freshman. The reaction throws me off a little, maybe because I'm not used to more innocent girls, and I have to ask, "How old are you, Effie?"

"Twenty-two," she replies breathlessly.

My eyes rove over her ambivalent expression, noticing slivers of guardedness behind her eyes. If I didn't know better, I'd say she's a virgin, too.

But I honestly can't imagine such a thing. A twenty-two-year-old virgin? Do those even exist? Maksim, my brain counters. That fucker was a good twenty-four before he did the deed. Of course, all of us brothers had already given up on him, assuming he was going for celibacy. Maybe it's the same with Effie.

"And how old are you?" she asks a little indignantly.

"Thirty-four."

She nods, and I can't help but admire her sex kitten allure. So sweet and so naughty without even knowing it. A deep, dark, sick part of me wants to taint the hell out of her. Invade every part of her. Penetrate and fill her up to the brim, claim her as mine.

Maybe Christian and my brothers were right to scold me. Of course, I've never been one to heed their advice. Why start now?

"You're older than I thought," she says, pursing her lips.

"Is that good or bad?" I ask.

She shrugs.

I narrow my eyes. "Just for the record. I'm old enough to know what I'm doing and why without the unnecessary drama and angst of a twenty-something dude. Yet, not too old to be a creep. Believe me, boys your age are looking for someone to take care of them. A second mommy. Men my age are looking for someone to care for and protect. It's a whole other ballgame. But enough flirting." I shut down the conversation before I get ahead of myself, heading into her kitchen.

Flipping the light switch, I stand motionless, absorbing all the pink vintage decor. It's the most feminine space I've seen in my entire life. The bad boy in me wants to roll around in it and fuck the floors. "I'll make coffee while you do whatever you need to so that you feel comfortable at the party."

Silence.

I hesitate for a moment, my stomach knotting before I lean back through the archway between the kitchen and the living room, adding, "Oh, and bring an overnight bag because it's dumping outside, and there's a chance we'll get snowed in over there tonight."

"I can't stay at your family's home overnight. Will there be enough rooms and beds for all of us?"

"You can stay in my room," I volunteer with an ear-to-ear grin, making her glow crimson. I chuckle, waving away her worry. "The ranch is huge with plenty of rooms. Don't worry about a thing, Blackbird. I've been known to be a gentleman on occasion."

"First stormy and now blackbird?"

"I'll explain in the car," I say with a wink. "Oh, and don't forget your guitar."

Chapter Eight

EFFIE

Silence engulfs us as we crunch through the snow and ice toward Rough & Ready Ranch. A part of me feels excited to finally see the place. I've heard so much about it from the romance readers and Lily, and I'm relieved to not spend Christmas alone, even if I'm not quite ready to admit this to Rock. I also can't deny the warmth he's put in my heart, refusing to let me spend the holidays alone. In a sense, he cares more about me than my own mother, both depressing and wildly attractive.

With this newfound warmth comes the sense that I'm slipping, and it scares the hell out of me. From pure disdain and annoyance the first two times I met him to something bordering on like and intrigue with a healthy smattering of lust. Okay, who am I fooling? The lust has always been there....from day one. But with each interaction, it gets harder to reign in, especially as disdain and annoyance give way to friendly affection.

I side-eye the rocker's drool-worthy profile, savoring the laid-back, sensual way he holds himself and moves through life. His gorgeous nonchalance makes my insides melt and throb. His generous lips captivate me, motivating crazy thoughts about how he tastes and how his hot, velvety tongue would feel sliding between my lips. And his muscular, lean build invites me to touch him, tracing his tattoos from one end to the other, lingering long and ravenously on every inch of skin in between. Even his cologne envelopes me like a warm hug, spicy and musky, and I want to wake up with the fragrance on my bedsheets and in my hair...on my skin and between my thighs.

Beware of bad-boy rockers. And cowboys, for that matter.

No matter how jaw-dropping this guy may be, I absolutely cannot fall for him. I steal another glance at him, trying to keep my breathing steady, but want shouts above every other thought in my head, drowning out logic, reason, and common sense. I have to stop thinking about him. My mind and body need a distraction, so I clear my throat, asking, "Why the new nickname 'blackbird'?"

A luscious smile captures his lips, enhancing their kissability, and his tongue darts out, sensually wetting his lower lip and making me think of all the other places I'd like to feel it lap and swirl my flesh.

"Well, obviously, because you're dainty and delicate, a little bird-like with your fast movements and excitable personality."

"I'm a good size twelve to fourteen. How is that dainty or delicate?" I scold, sounding more like a kindergarten teacher than I care to admit. Usually, I share as little as possible about myself with others, especially my dress size. After all, trust is earned, not given. So either the egg nog still impairs my filter despite the black coffee Rock force-fed me. Or a part of me hopes to scare the bad boy away before that slipping feeling gives way to falling.

He shrugs, biting his lower lip. "Put whatever number you like on it. It won't change the fact you're sexy as hell."

I frown, grimacing. "Really? You can have any woman you want on this planet. Why would you look twice at a curvy girl like me?"

"First off, I can't have any woman I want on this planet, or our evening would look quite different," he says, shooting me a simmering gaze that makes me breathe faster. "Second, who are you to judge what turns me on? Aren't I allowed to have my own opinion? Curvy, sexy, busty, hot-as-fuck minxes included?"

My cheeks blossom with heat. "You're clearly a master at objectification. Have you ever thought there's more to women than sex?" I sigh, looking down at the hands I twist in my lap.

He cocks his head and eyes me with an amused expression. "Obviously. What kind of question is that?"

I frown. "This is exactly why I avoid bad boy types like you...and my dad. You're more trouble than you're worth."

"Okay, you've alluded to your father being a rocker twice now. Are you ready to tell me who he is?" Rock asks gently.

I freeze for a moment. But then a thought hits me. *What can it hurt?* After all, he could very well hear about it from Dee or one of his sisters at the party tonight. I'm still kicking myself for being so forthright at the romance readers club.

"Sax Gunner."

Rock nods, biting the inside of his bottom lip. He doesn't look shocked, which makes me think one of his sisters or maybe Dee has already spilled the tea.

"Nice of you to stick me in the same category with him, but I'm not even close. Sax Gunner's in the Rock 'n' Roll Hall of Fame."

Shaking my head, I say, "It's even worse you looking up to him."

"Have you ever reached out to him? Gotten his side of the story?"

I exhale sharply. "Absolutely not." As soon as the words escape my lips, I realize how unenlightened they sound.

"Can I ask you to withhold judgment about Sax? At least until you hear his side of the story?"

"There's no way I'm ever going to hear his side of the story," I retort. "I want nothing to do with him, just like he's wanted nothing to do with me for more than two decades now." I use my hands to gesture as I talk.

A long stretch of silence follows. "So, back to blackbird..." Rock finally says, breaking the thick atmosphere in the Bronco.

I nod.

"Of course, your black hair made me think of the nickname, although at first, I was going more along the lines of a raven. But then, I heard you sing again and knew I couldn't use an endearment for something that squawks and bawks. Blackbirds are songbirds, each species singing a unique tune. That suited you better, and then from there, I thought of The Beatles song "Blackbird," which fits you so damn well, it gives me chills to think about the lyrics."

I begrudgingly admit, "I love that song."

"Do you know the lyrics? Because it's one I want to sing with you at the party tonight."

I sigh long and loudly. "I still can't believe you're making me do this...all of this."

"Do you always have to be such a party pooper?" my Lazarus asks, eyeing me seriously.

"Party pooper!" I exclaim with more force than I mean to, making him tense up momentarily. A shit-eating grin captures his face like he expects me to punch him. The thought tempts me. "This isn't even my party."

"It is now," he growls throatily. "You can either enjoy the experience and make the most of it or pout and moan about how you don't belong."

"But I don't!"

"It's not about you," he counters in gruff tones. "Hell, most of life isn't about either one of us. We are here to bring joy and love to others, and none of us realistically has much time. So, wasting it is a bad idea."

"Is this the new evolved Rock?" I question skeptically.

"It's the Rock who's decided to take account of his actions and quit blaming others for everything that's happened in my life. Who's traded in drinking his life away for trying to give back to others...quit missing the forest for the trees in a sense."

"I could almost think you were a decent guy with a speech like that. Until I remind myself a little over two months ago, you were passed out in my backyard and then pissing on it."

"Enough," the tattooed rocker grits between clenched teeth, and the cab of the Bronco goes silent. "Damn, girl. You know how to suck the life out of everything..."

The words hit harder than they should. Not so much because of the deliverer but because of how they echo down through time. My mom always said that my birth ruined her life, stealing her opportunities and future. Rationally, I understand Rock didn't mean to stumble over one of my triggers, but that doesn't make it smart any less. Looking at his tight, tense face, I have to admit I may have stumbled over one of his triggers, too.

Silence.

Finally, Rock's growly tenor pulls me back from my thoughts as he breaks into the opening lyrics of "Blackbird," settling into a key we can both comfortably hold. It's an invitation and a white flag. Despite lingering anger, I concentrate on his soulful timbre and how he slides over notes, infusing them with heart, depth, and passion.

After indulging in this auditory pleasure for a few moments, I tap the first beat of each measure on my leg, keeping gentle time as I sing along, dancing above his notes, just out of reach before crashing down into his lush tones with a sexy assertiveness I've never found expression for before. A part of me never wants this to end.

"That's you," he says at the end, reaching over the console momentarily to squeeze my hands, still fisted in my lap. The warmth of his flesh ignites delicious little sparks along the backs of my hands and into my wrists and forearms. I wonder, trying to catch my breath, what his hands could inspire the rest of my body to feel. I can't let this happen...*under any circumstances*.

Silence invades the cab for another long stretch, and I second-guess myself. If I keep acting like this, I will end up alone on Christmas. And although I learned to deal with this inevitability from an early age, I prefer the option Rock offers instead.

Clearing my throat, I say begrudgingly, "Thank you for stopping to get me today and bringing me with you. I must admit this is better than spending the holidays alone and drunk."

He nods, his expression serious. "I thought you'd eventually come around to the idea. Besides, I can second you on the alone and drunk part. It always sounds better when standing in line at the bar or liquor store than praying to the porcelain god."

"About that... Are you an alcoholic? I hate to ask, but after the bush incident, I have questions."

"Fair enough," he says, frowning. "I haven't drunk a drop of liquor since waking up with thorn bushes in my back and your voice in my ears. I'm an active member of Alcoholics Anonymous, and I plan on staying that way, although not everybody's too happy about it."

Chapter Nine

EFFIE

I ask, "Who's not happy about it?"

"Mainly the Lowlifes. And I can't really blame them because our songs are all about drugs and drinking, and our fans are all neck-deep in that culture. But that comeuppance in October has stuck with me, and I'd rather not go back to that half-life I was living before. Now, that said, I don't think you would have classed me before as an alcoholic. I didn't drink every night or anything along those lines. But I relied on it as a crutch to help me regulate my emotions, and that's a slippery slope."

Guilt convicts me. "You mean like I was doing when you showed up at the house earlier?"

"Maybe," he replies, side-eyeing me. "You tell me. Were you drinking because you were lonely? If so, I get it. That's mostly why I drank, along with wanting to take the edge off before social events. I'm shyer than most people realize. I'm also kind of a needy, sensitive guy. And when I don't get enough human companionship and physical attention...or in the case of October, when I'm fucking betrayed, I kind of fall apart. Alcohol seemed to make sense at the time, but looking back, I realize it only turned the downward spiral into the ultimate toilet flush. But I'll never regret the outcome—you—right when I needed to see you most. I've never believed in a higher power. But between meeting you in October and how we sing together, it's hard to believe this is just some cosmic accident."

His words make my heart thrill and expand, and they also fill me with trepidation. Clearing my throat, I point out, "That's a lot to ask of one woman, you know."

"What do you mean?"

"To keep you sober and religious."

He laughs. "Blackbird, if it was up to me, you'd be my religion..."

I exhale sharply.

"I know, I know. I'm saying stuff that's not socially appropriate. And I guess if I ran it by my therapist, she'd tell me I'm being co-dependent or some shit like that. But rest assured, I'd never ask anything of you I wouldn't give wholeheartedly in return."

We need a change of topic because this is heading way too deep, and I'm not entirely sure I believe him. After all, can an inveterate rocker with groupies throwing themselves all over him really settle down?

I squeeze my hands in my lap, and he glances at me, his turquoise eyes overflowing with tenderness and warmth.

I ask. "Were Lily and Turner really serious about cowboy songs for Wyatt?"

He laughs. "Is that your way of saying I've gone too far?"

"It's my way of saying we need a change of subject."

"Noted," he says with a frown. "In answer to your question, absolutely. Dad'll eat that shit up. Want to give 'Happy Trails' a whirl?"

"Yes," I answer, breathing a sigh of relief. I need time to process everything he's told me and to see whether his actions match his words. If there's one thing my childhood experiences have taught me: talk is cheap. And promises are bargain basement valued.

"You want to lead?" Rock asks, his face unreadable.

"Sure."

I begin, and this time, we get a little more playful, gliding over each other's notes and trying new things. The experimentation leads to more stops and something akin to actually practicing, with several laughs in between. It feels good. Like it's supposed to be this way. For the first time, I see how we could work together, live together, and love together. I stare at him for a moment, and his eyes flicker to mine, his jaw tightening.

"Sorry," I apologize, furrowing my brows and looking away.

"No need to apologize. I like looking at you, too."

"Why?" I ask boldly despite the slight shake in my voice.

He shrugs. "I don't know. Maybe because it feels right..."

I roll my eyes, my hands fidgeting and my eyes rounding. "There you go with the stupid bad-boy pickup lines." I can't hide the derisive edge to my voice.

He laughs. "I'm going to be very blunt because otherwise, I don't think you'll believe me. But please don't take this the wrong way or think I'm an egomaniac or anything. Promise?"

"I can't make that promise."

He shakes his head. "You're one tough cookie. You know that?"

I shrug.

"With looks like mine, tattoos like mine, jobs like mine... You get where I'm going with this?"

I roll my eyes, frowning.

"I don't need one-liners. Never have. Honestly, women use one-liners on me. So rest assured, whatever I say to you—

no matter how fucking cheesy, due to inexperience—is sincere and coming from the deepest part of me."

My cheeks flush. "You are so full of shit."

"What?" His voice rises at the end.

"It would be better to drive in silence than listen to this. Whatever this is. Can you go a full conversation without pointing out that women adore you?"

His face looks dumbstruck. Although he opens his mouth, no words come out.

Anger washes over me as I mock his voice, mimicking, "I don't need one-liners because I never have to come on to a woman. They always come on to me."

"I'm going to quit talking around you because you take everything I say the wrong way, twisting it into something bad. Something I don't mean."

"The problem is you're just so full of yourself. I mean, seriously."

"And you've made up your mind about me, which means you have to twist and turn everything I say and do until it fits your image of me. What's the fucking point under those circumstances?"

I try to bite my tongue, but I can't help myself. "If the shoe fits..."

"Think what you like about me. All I know is our voices go together, for God only knows what reason. Maybe this is the universe biting me in the ass for all of those years of havoc I caused..."

"Whatever you say, Smuggy."

"Smuggy? What's that supposed to mean?" he grumbles.

"If you're going to have nicknames for me, I'm entitled to do the same."

He laughs darkly. "So, smuggy like egotistical, narcissistic?"

"Bingo."

He pumps the brakes to bring the Bronco to a stop next to the line of trucks and other four-wheel-drive vehicles. "Alright, I'll give you a five-second head start, but then I'm white-washing the shit out of you."

"What?"

"Five..."

"Rock?"

"Even if it means dragging you out of this damn Bronco. Four..."

My breath catches in my throat, and my heart pounds against my ribs as one look his way lets me know the rocker's serious.

"I'd like to see you try!" I challenge, flinging the car door open and running out into the fluffy white howl of the snowstorm as I hear Rock call, "Three..."

Chapter Ten

ROCK

S hards of ice cling to the inside of my shirt and around my neck, raising goosebumps over the flesh of my torso. I breathe hard, still laughing as I open the door to the ranch, trudging through with a snow-covered blackbird pinned against my torso, my right arm a steel band around her curvy waist, and her feet off the ground. The lights from the massive Christmas tree twinkle, and heat from the room hits me as faces turn, rushing from the kitchen and dining area into the living room to greet us.

"I brought trouble with me," I grumble matter-of-factly, setting Blackbird on her feet gently so that she can begin shaking the snow out of her hair and from her clothes.

"Did you two fall outside or something?" Roxy asks, laughing and rushing forward to hesitantly air hug us both.

"Nope, just white-washed the shit out of each other," I chuckle, shooting a too-warm look at Effie and making her blush.

Roxy offers to take our jackets, and I hand her my flannel-lined black leather jacket with a "thank you." Effie peels off her snow-crusted black leather jacket, black and white skull scarf, and matching mittens, handing them unceremoniously to Roxy. "I'm putting these in the washroom to dethaw," my sister-in-law says, making her braids dance as she moves.

Roxy walks through the kitchen into the mudroom as the family crowds around us. Christian's ambivalent eyes and frown catch my attention as he eyes me and my renter, shaking his head. But Lily, Alex, and Jess rush forward, wrapping their arms around Effie and making her feel right at home. She briefly turns her warm lavender eyes towards me, "thank you" written all over them. My heart expands, knowing I did the right thing.

Dee greets me with a side hug, brushing some clinging snow from my flannel shirt, which I wear unbuttoned with a Stray Cats T-shirt underneath.

"Fancy seeing you two together," the redhead says with a mischievous grin.

"You and I both know you had something to do with that," I growl, trying to play it grumpy. But I can't help the smile that seizes my face. Still, I can't have Dee jumping to any conclusions, either. I whisper, "Nice try. But we fight like cats and dogs. I wouldn't be surprised if she actually hates me."

Dee's brows skim her hairline. "Seriously? After your duet the other day? You guys were amazing onstage. It's like your voices were made for each other."

I kick the floor in front of me, looking down. "Maybe, but Effie makes it otherwise clear she despises me. And honestly, I'm not sure I can be with someone who's so judgmental and uptight."

"That's too bad," she says, the corners of her mouth turning downward. "I guess it was worth a try. All I know is you're a good man who deserves good things."

Sometimes, I think Dee's the only person who sees me this way. Glancing around the room, frowns on a couple more of my brothers' faces confirm this conclusion. But Dee makes me want to rise to the occasion and prove her right. I would feel the same way about Effie if she didn't make every word and action of mine into a foregone conclusion.

"Most people think of me as irresponsible, immature, and reckless around here...teetering on the not so coveted black sheep of the family role. So, your confidence in me is appreciated."

She laughs. "Actually, I think that title sits squarely on Holden's shoulders now. But we'll see what happens when he gets out." Her voice contains a wistfulness that I always hear when she talks about my bro.

"You always do choose to see the best in people," I half-grimace, half-smile.

"Well, everyone deserves a second chance. Of course, I've lost count of how many your family has given you over the years. Wyatt's been especially patient." She refers to my hell-raising teen years and early twenties when I bounded from rehab facility to rehab facility, broken intermittently by bouts of running away, indigence, and jail time. I could never truly wrap my head around the fact I deserved to be at Rough & Ready Ranch, and God only knows how Wyatt put up with me. But that old cowboy taught me what pure, unconditional love is, and he saved my life in the process.

"You never mince words, do you, Dee?"

She shakes her head. "Anyway, sorry about the whole guitar thing and making you get up early. Effie said a few things at the romance readers group that put me in match-maker mode. That's all."

"Yeah, like what?"

"That she has a thing for tattooed cowboys, which obviously brought you to mind since Christian's already taken."

I mutter darkly before I can catch myself, "Christian better stay in his lane..." I still remember the way Effie looked at him back in October, and it pisses me off to no end.

Dee laughs. "Jealous much?"

From across the room, where she stands chatting excitedly with my sisters-in-law, Effie looks in my direction, doing a double-take at the way I still have my arm around Dee. Her lavender eyes darken and narrow, and her face tightens.

"If I didn't know better, I'd say you're not the only jealous person in this room," Dee observes with a chuckle.

I shrug. "Doesn't matter if she persists in always seeing the worst side of me." Still, I like the validation Effie's expression and Dee's comment give my heart.

"There's a thin line between love and hate, you know."

"So everyone tells me," I mutter.

I let go of Dee, shrugging casually and nodding towards the door. "I've got to grab our guitars before the cold starts snapping strings."

"You brought your guitars?" she asks, a happy smile crossing her lips.

"Yep, music is the only way we get along. Otherwise, we more or less want to kill each other. At least Effie does."

A few minutes later, I reappear, setting the guitars by the door and shivering from tackling the trip without a coat. Alex sees the cases and calls across the crowd of family, "Shoot, if I'd have known, I would have brought my cello."

I shrug. "Sorry, Sis, but I wasn't sure how successful I'd be at getting this thing out of her house and over here. Next time, though."

"Will there be a next time?" Effie asks, arching her lovely black eyebrow and frowning.

"More than that, if I get my way. And you can ask anyone around here. I'm pretty damn good at that."

She purses her lips, shaking her head, and silently mouthing, "Smuggy."

More than one brother shifts his weight, nodding slowly. Their concerned expressions tell me they're still worried I'm somehow going to hurt the minx. If only they knew she's elevated tongue-slashing me to an art form.

Pops comes forward with his best friend, Roxy's grandpa, Uncle Billy, at his side. I lean down, putting each man in a bear hug in turn.

"You're looking better than usual, son. Almost respectable," Pops says with a pleased grin.

"I haven't had a drink in two months, thanks to her," I say, nodding towards Effie.

She shakes her head, retorting, "Thanks to a pyracanthas bush."

Pops's eyebrows raise, and the corners of his mouth turn down ever so slightly.

"It's a long story best kept for another time," I reply.

"Good to stay off the bottle," Billy chimes in. "Never done nobody any good."

"Ain't that the truth," I say, removing my cowboy hat to swipe a hand through my brown hair. "After dinner, Effie and I will sing some duets together. Some people seem to think our voices go well together, although definitely not our personalities. Anyway, think on any requests you might have."

"Logan and Jess were telling me about your duet just yesterday. I'm excited to hear you two together. They said it was like a match made in heaven."

"Sir, I don't know much about heaven, but I'm pretty darn sure it includes Effie's voice."

Pops leans in closer, and I bend down towards him. "You sound smitten, son."

"I could be, although it's clearly not in my best interest," I confess, rubbing the place on my chest over my heart and casting a long, wistful glance toward our topic of conversation.

"It never is. But with the right one, it's worth it." He winks.

"Right one? Not so much." I shake my head. But the

tanned, wizened cowboy doesn't look especially convinced. *What do Dee and he see that I don't?*

Billy's face looks solemn, but he nods his agreement.

The guitars remain propped against the wall near the front door while we eat dinner. My sisters-in-law have outdone themselves with an epic spread that could feed an entire army. Sweet potatoes with tiny marshmallows and brown sugar, mounds of homemade dressing, and red-skinned mashed potatoes with gravy. Turkey and ham cooked to perfection, and every side you can imagine, from green bean casserole to cranberry relish, cheese and broccoli bake to housemaid croissants and rolls from Cricket's bakery.

Cricket is Christian's wife, and they recently had triplets, giving them a run for their money. Christian looks serious every time I glance his way, but he's too busy taking care of the babies with his adorable wife for a threatening older brother talk. The same goes for Logan, who focuses on keeping Jess comfortable and happy in her very pregnant state. As for Turner and Hawk, neither has anything to say nor does Maksim, Flynn, Fletcher, or Ridge. They're all around my age or younger and don't feel the same impetus to keep everyone in line.

Chapter Eleven

ROCK

After our bellies are filled to the brim and cookies, pies, and ice cream have made the rounds, I grab Effie's hand, catching her eye with a warm glint before we make our way to the place in front of the tree where two tall stools from the kitchen bar sit. She takes a seat, and I beeline for our guitars.

We uncase and tune without speaking. When I shoot a look in her direction, I see nervousness bubbling beneath the surface despite her tough facade. Grabbing her arm and rubbing my thumb sensually across the cowgirl on the inside of her wrist, I say, "Nothing to be nervous about. Everyone in this room loves us...the both of us."

Instead of pulling her arm away from me and hissing out some mean comeback, she smiles, her eyes warming and her shoulders noticeably relaxing. I could get used to making her respond this way, but first, I have to figure out how to make lightning strike twice. She's usually far too guarded around me for such an exchange.

"We're going to take it one song at a time and see where this goes. Okay, Blackbird?"

"Alright, Smuggy."

"'Happy Trails'?"

She nods. "Always good to start strong."

Leaning back on my stool, my eyes flutter towards Dee who holds my cell phone in hand, ready to record everything. As I warned Skates, the sound quality won't be great. But I don't want to make Effie self-conscious by letting her know what I'm doing. Yeah, she may be a little pissed off later, but it'll be well worth it to send my producer unguarded, candid recordings of whatever this magic is going on between us.

Unlike our previous duets, which happened on the fly and completely improvised, we launch into this one with a plan, emphasizing each other's strengths and drawing the meaning in the lyrics out. I don't know if my heart will ever stop thrilling at how her luscious vocals shimmer over the top of mine or how her lavender eyes follow me, reading my mind, heart, and soul as we jump off the same musical cliffs together. Somehow always landing in the same spot.

At the end, the air feels thick and heavy, and it takes a moment before the family starts clapping and hollering. My gaze holds Effie's, and I want her. Not solely with my body but also my heart and my soul. I need her in a way I've never needed anyone before...more basic to existence than water or air. Leaning towards her, she draws closer, probably because she thinks I'm about to whisper the next song's title in her ear.

Instead, I say softly, "Stormy, would you be too terribly mad at me...if I fell in love with you?"

Her cheeks darken, but she doesn't pull back. I raise an eyebrow questioningly, and she presses her lips together, her mind working. "You shouldn't do that," she whispers back.

"Why not?"

"Because I don't want to break your heart."

"Hell, girl, that's already done," I confess, my voice raw.

What's the point of being able to get any girl I want except the one I need?

"If y'all insist on tête-à-tête's between every song, this concert's going to take all night," my bull-riding brother, Zane, calls from the back. He lounges in his chair, his arm protectively around his wife, Birdie, a former rodeo queen.

Next to the pair, sits another brother, Flynn, every bit the cowboy with his button-down shirt, neat fade and ebony skin. His fingers are tangled with Jasmine's, his Latina paralegal-turned-wife. Flynn nods in agreement, adding, "Maybe you two can't get enough of each other. But the rest of us need more than a song every half hour."

"Alright, alright," I laugh, looking down momentarily, trying to figure out our next song.

"How about 'Tainted Love?'" Ridge grumbles from the back, a feral mountain man and outdoorsman, from his unkempt beard to his anti-social frown. He's never had luck with the ladies or even civilization, so his request is anything but surprising.

Fletcher shakes his head. "Too depressing even for me." My Army cardiology brother has been in a torturous, on-again, off-again relationship for far too long. He's also usually too busy for family functions, hence Christmas Eve versus Christmas Day scheduling. "If you're taking requests, how about Chris Isaak's *Wicked Games?*"

"And then, after that, Johnny Cash's *Ring of Fire,*" Flynn adds.

"Actually, June Carter Cash wrote that one," I remind with a nod. I look at Effie, my brow raised.

She nods, quirking her mouth and furrowing her brow. I'd give an arm and a leg for her thoughts right now. Instead, I strum out the familiar chords, launching into Chris Isaak's lonely, desperado vocals. I get this request often at the

Lowlifes' shows, so it fits comfortably, like my favorite pair of steel-toed combat boots or my softest flannel shirt.

As we sing, we draw closer to one another. It's as if our souls strain to be together despite ourselves, and I can't help but wonder what could happen between us if she didn't insist on being so stubborn. By the end of our concert, a thick lump lodges in my throat, and my heart flings around in my chest, frantic to keep up with the dark, sensual thoughts in my head.

Need is a whole other kind of monster with Effie, not one I'm certain I can control. Fortunately, she's got enough self-control—or hatred—for both of us.

Everyone gathers around, complimenting us and talking about their favorite songs. Of course, they're my family, but the level of support still tells me I'm right about my gut instinct when it comes to Effie and me.

Dee comes up beside me after the girls grab Effie, heading off to chat and giggle.

"Did you get a couple of tracks?" I ask.

She nods, smiling. "I can't vouch for their quality, and I'm guessing there's a fair amount of ambient noise to contend with. But hopefully, that gives your producer friend a better idea of your sound."

"Thanks, baby girl."

"You know, once Holden gets out of prison, he won't take too kindly to that nickname," she warns with a smile. All of my brothers consider me a bit too flirtatious around their women. "And Effie doesn't seem to appreciate us in close proximity, either," she adds, nodding towards my singing partner, who stares holes through us before my gaze captures hers and she looks away.

"Thanks, Dee."

"You're welcome. Now, let's see how bad the weather's getting."

Stepping outside into the chill of the night air, billows of white cover the ground with seasonal festivity. But the brunt of the storm hasn't blown in yet, which means my Bronco's more than capable of getting Effie home.

Before we depart, I discreetly send the tracks to Skates. I should listen to them and do some editing. But he's received raw audio from me before, and I feel so strongly about our duets that I can't wait for his feedback.

After saying our goodbyes and departing in the Bronco, Effie gushes about the wonderful evening and how much fun she had. Seeing her like this and knowing I had something to do with it warms my heart.

When we reach her place, I escort her to the porch, but she refuses the hand I offer to keep her from slipping. She stands in the doorway, her cheeks rosy, staring up at me, a strange mixture of desire and fear swirling in her eyes. Anticipation hangs on her lips, which she licks slowly, inviting me to kiss her. But God only knows how she'd react to that. And there is the little matter of freezing my ass off.

I ask, "Mind if I come in and warm up for a few?"

The conflict in her expression intensifies, even though I can tell by how her eyes rove over me that she's thinking at least part of what I'm thinking.

Taking a deep breath to quell the nervousness inside, a feeling I'm not used to, I reassure her, "Don't worry, Blackbird. I promise to be a gentleman."

I swear, she looks a little disappointed by the statement, which confuses the hell out of me. *What in the fuck does this woman want?*

She bids me come in with a begrudging shrug. Stomping my feet in the entryway on the welcome mat, I say, "Thank you. It's colder than a witch's tit out there."

She laughs, her eyes rounding at my crudeness.

"Sorry, it's not often I'm in the presence of a lady."

"A lady?" she laughs, raising her eyebrows as she flips light switches around the house.

"One look at your kitchen tells me you're a lady, which makes our initial meeting all the more embarrassing now that I think back on it," I confess, my eyes following her and hungrily devouring her from behind as she plays with the thermostat. "Can I get a fire going in the hearth for you?" I ask, nodding towards the modest nineteen thirteen-style Craftsman fireplace.

"Oh! That sounds so cozy. I've never made one yet because...well, honestly, I don't know how. Do you?"

"Of course. How do you think we cowboys stay warm during cattle drives and all? It's not like we're packing mini, solar-powered heaters."

"Cattle drives? Seriously? I figured the hat and boots meant you worked outdoors, but that's some crazy eighteen-hundreds type stuff."

"Cattle need moving no matter what century you live in," I call over my shoulder. "Do you have some newspapers or other kindling I can use?"

"No newspaper. But I have some of those newsprint flyers that come in the mail. Will those work?"

I nod, working on stacking the wood together in a tepee formation while she heads into the kitchen to retrieve the kindling she mentioned. I project my voice, continuing, "Pops is the real deal, and Rough & Ready Ranch always has been and remains a working cattle ranch, although my brother Zane took over as foreman from Wyatt a while ago. Pops promised each of us boys that if we kept our shit together and became upstanding citizens, he'd give us each a ten-acre parcel to build our own cabin and work the land. Or at least keep it up. I'm surprised he held up his deal with me because I was a hellion as a teen, and I really put him through it. But now I realize he's the lighthouse that brought me safely through every storm without crashing on the rocks. It may sound cheesy to you, but with my childhood, I needed that big time."

"Tell me about it," she says bitterly.

"What?"

"Tough childhoods."

"I'm a good listener, you know, if you'd ever like to talk things out," I offer as she hands me a large pile of newsprint mailers.

"Not so much. I hate dwelling on the past," she replies nervously, biting her lush lower lip hard. *Does she ever truly let her guard down to trust anyone?* "Can I get you a hot cocoa or tea while you work on that?" she asks in a buttery voice.

I swallow loudly, "Hot cocoa sounds amazing. Thank you."

"Marshmallows or the Effie way?"

I laugh, "The Effie way, of course." Rubbing the place over my heart, I wonder if I'll regret my decision.

"Excuse my manners. May I take your jacket and hat?" she asks.

I realize I haven't asked to take hers, either. "Only if I can get your coat and scarf?"

She nods, and I settle into the strange realization she actually wants me to stay around for a while. Amazing what loneliness around the holidays can do, even to the toughest Grinch.

Chapter Twelve

EFFIE

What am I doing? Inviting Rockwell Landry in. Taking his jacket and hat and offering him a hot drink? These are not the moves of a woman who knows she needs to say goodnight before things get confusing and complicated. But a compelling, powerful part of me, namely all of my flesh, does want to confuse and complicate the heck out of this situation.

Is this how my mother ended up single and knocked up by my father?

I shake my head, acknowledging a world of difference between me and my mom. Listen to her, and you'd think everything in life happened to her, that there was nothing she could do about it, and she was and forever remains a perennial victim. However, I am a grown-ass woman who can take care of myself.

Until now, I've chalked myself up as not the relationship type. No man's really ever done it for me. But Rockwell Landry's another story. What would it feel like to let him bring the simmering feelings he awakens in me to a boil? Curiosity and lust grip me.

As a modern, responsible, sophisticated woman, I should be able to have sex with him, let him pop my cherry, and avoid getting attached, right? It sounds so good on the surface... But the best-laid plans have a way of unraveling. I glance guiltily back in the living room, where Rock kneels before the fireplace. Am I seriously considering having sex with this man?

Beware bad-boy rockers. I'm tired of living from a place of fear. Why couldn't the mantra be something like *Beware of badass kindergarten teachers?* The thought makes me chuckle as I focus on making hot cocoa.

While I heat water in a kettle, I pour the rest of my eggnog down the sink. I don't need it, and my house guest certainly doesn't.

A deep voice rumbles behind me. "I hope you're not doing that on account of me."

I shrug. "I'm doing it on account of both of us."

He eyes the room inquisitively for a moment. "The way you decorate is so damn girlie."

"Is it a problem?"

"Nope," he replies, shaking his head. "Although feel like a courtier who snuck into the queen's chambers. You know, kind of naughty, like I'm not supposed to be here."

"That's funny, considering this is your property."

"Yeah, but you and I both know by rights I owe you a twenty-four-hour written notice. Which reminds me. Where did the kittens go?"

I thumb over my shoulder towards the back of the house, explaining, "I've got them shut up in my bathroom. You know, so you won't break out in hives."

"Thanks. It's not an especially attractive look."

"Rockwell Landry ever looking unattractive? How could that be possible?" I sneer sarcastically, grabbing two mugs from the cabinet and setting them on the counter.

"Once you've made up your mind, that's it. No way to change it?" he asks next to me.

I anticipated a snarky comment instead of a question, so I fall silent, thinking about an answer. Wetting my lips, I finally say, "Well, my first impressions are almost always right. So, why second-guess myself? Second-guessing myself and letting my guard down are recipes for the same thing—getting hurt." I fill each mug with hot water before adding hot cocoa mix packets.

"Not giving anyone a second chance will also lead to you getting hurt, you know."

I raise a quizzical eyebrow.

"Because most people are way more complicated than a first impression. And if you always stop at your initial judgment, you're not giving them the chance to prove you wrong anyway. Or become better people. Talk about a negatively reinforcing behavior. I'm an expert on those, by the way."

"Why does this revelation not surprise me?" Retrieving a can of whipped cream from the refrigerator, I top each drink with a dollop of the white, cloudy stuff before grabbing the bag of crushed candy canes I keep in the cabinet over the stove and sprinkling a pinch on each.

He frowns, pressing his lips together. "You seriously keep a bag of crushed candy canes in your house?" he licks his lips as his eyes drop to the mug I hand him. Our fingers brush, causing heated sparks to cascade into my wrist and down my arm. *Dammit! Why is my body doing this to me?*

My cheeks burn because I can't tell whether he's staring at the mug or my boobs. Either way, he looks ravenous.

"Why are you blushing?" he asks. "My crushed candy cane comment too much for you?"

I stop, putting my hand on my hip. I feel another round of uncontrollable truth-telling coming on. "No, I caught you staring at the...girls. At least, I'm pretty sure you were."

He smiles, looking at the ceiling and briefly closing his eyes. "Guilty as charged. You know, for a sweet, little, innocent thing, you don't shy away from dropping some truth bombs."

I grab my mug, nodding towards the living room, where I can hear the fire crackling. "Most people would not class me as sweet or innocent with the tattoos, the hair, the makeup... what you referred to earlier as an edgy rocker look."

He chuckles. "You've got it all wrong. Everything about you exudes innocent, sunshiny wholesomeness, despite your attempts at a jaded outer facade. I mean, your tattoos are all 1950s-inspired, Stormy."

Annoyance seizes me, and I frown because I know he's right. Still, it doesn't make me anymore willing to admit it.

Swallowing hard, he adds, "And I'm good with that because what I'm interested in goes well below skin deep. I'm trying to figure out your heart and your soul. You know, penetrate down to the core of you."

My cheeks blaze. "Nice choice of verbs, there, Smuggy."

He chuckles. "So what? I'm supposed to pretend I'm a fucking monk and hide my attraction for you?"

I shrug. " I'm not relationship material if that helps."

"Not relationship material?" he repeats with a grimace. "Nobody really is. It's something you have to work at."

"I mean, I'm not interested in them. I don't need anybody."

"I may not know you well. But I highly doubt that."

"Why do you say that?" I ask, watching him press his lips tightly together. I motion for him to sit on the couch in front of the fireplace, and he does so carefully to avoid spilling his hot cocoa. He puts enough distance between us to be respectable. It both relieves and disappoints me.

"By the way you look at me. Say what you like, but your eyes clearly convey you want me...the way I want you. And want comes with need. Is that so wrong?"

My heart flings itself pathetically against my ribcage, but I try to play off my racing pulse with an uninterested shrug. Clearing my throat, I concentrate on keeping my voice even. "I guess not. We're all animals, after all."

He smiles. "I knew you were going to say something like that."

"Reading my mind now? That's quite a talent.

"Trying to get to know you is all. But you don't make that easy."

"Why should I?" I ask, a little more passionately than I mean to. "People have always, always let me down. I put no trust in anyone because they're ultimately just looking out for themselves."

Chapter Thirteen

EFFIE

Rock's eyes narrow, and he carefully sips his hot chocolate. "If I didn't know better, I'd say you were raised by a narcissist, which would make your guardedness and current conclusions understandable though still wrong."

His words pierce me, followed by a flash of red, hot anger. "Don't talk about what you don't know. My mother's a good woman. She sacrificed everything to have me."

"Every decision in life comes with sacrifices. But I'm sure you realize you paid her back a thousand-fold by turning into an amazing daughter she can be proud of. Right?"

My throat feels thick, and my lips dangerously close to quivering. *What in the fuck is happening to me?* The backs of my eyes sting as I nearly let down my guard at his words. But I can't do this. Not with him. Not with anyone. Who is he to pretend he knows what my mom and I went through?

"If I need a therapist, I'll hire a therapist. Enough with the unsolicited advice." I blow on my hot chocolate before testing its temperature, trying hard to hide the tremble in my hands and arms as emotion continues to well, threatening to lay me bare and vulnerable in front of a man who can't be trusted.

Rock surrenders, saying, "Alright, alright. You caught me. As a former foster kid, I've talked with more therapists and social workers than you've probably met in your entire life. And I've been reading a ton of self-help books and doing the whole AA thing, which encourages me to be more reflective. It has a tendency to bleed onto the lives of others through well-intentioned, though unsolicited, advice."

"You know what they say about the road to hell..." I frown.

"Stormy, I know more about the road to hell than you ever will. The guards lining it greet me by first name."

My eyes narrow. "That would make a great song lyric.

He chuckles, his eyes lingering on my lips.

"What?"

"You've got..." he sets his mug down on the coffee table in front of the couch before leaning forward. Palming my cheek, he run his thumb in a slow, sensual sweep over my lower lip. "A little whipped cream." He brings his thumb to his mouth, sensually licking it and awakening the intense throb between my legs once more. My cheek and lip burn from his touch, and need grips me.

I turn toward the coffee table, setting down my mug, and his face is inches from mine when I look back. His musky, spicy smell snakes around me, squeezing the breath from my lungs and the reason from my head.

His hand comes up to palm my cheek, and he strokes it, staring intensely into my eyes as our gazes mingle, brimming with want. Closing the distance, his soft, kissable lips cover mine. A deep growl rumbles from his chest as I move closer, settling into his warm, firm embrace. His mouth moves slowly and sensually over mine, taking his time and teasing me until I feel like my heart will explode.

"Do you want to kiss me or not?" I whisper breathlessly as I chase his lips, which nip and tease mine.

He chuckles. "Are you interested in a relationship or what?" he asks, raising his eyebrows.

"I don't know. But does it matter?"

"Yeah, if I fall for you, it fucking matters. Bad boy or not, I don't enjoy getting my heart broken." His cell phone vibrates in his pants pocket, but he ignores it.

"Don't fall for me then," I reply, crashing my mouth into his and sitting forward so I'm almost in his lap.

He wraps his arms more tightly around me, finishing the job of pulling me against him and onto his legs, seated sideways. His head drops to the crook of my neck as he showers me in tiny, mind-numbing kisses and swipes of his hot tongue. His fingers slide across my back, squeezing and caressing me.

I whimper, settling into his heat and all-encompassing strength, logic banished from my brainwaves as I let my head fall back in surrender. All I know is I want him more than I've ever wanted anyone, which means I can't think of a better man to take my virginity—*bad-boy rock star or not*.

Rock's cell phone vibrates again. "Fuck," he growls. "Whoever's calling can wait."

He brings his hands into my hair and his mouth to the shell of my ear. His tongue traces its shape before descending to the lobe, which he nibbles and plays with. "What do you need from me?" His voice has a rawness that makes me hug his neck more desperately. Everything about him tastes, smells, sounds, looks, and feels so good. I'm starved for him, ravenous as a bear waking up from hibernation.

"Everything," I sigh.

He swallows hard. "Virgin or not? I need to know."

"Virgin," I say with a tremulous sigh. "Is it that obvious?"

"Kind of," he answers distantly. His whole body tenses, and his hands and lips freeze on me.

"What's wrong, Rock?"

His cell phone vibrates again, but the rocker seems determined to ignore it.

Leveling his gaze on me, he asks, "Are you going to fucking hate me for hurting you? And taking that from you?" He leans back, looking me in the eyes, his face grave. "I mean, one minute you despise me, then the next you kiss me and want more. I'm confused, like really confused right now, Effie. As much as I'd like to get to know you better, having sex with you would mean something to me. So, if you're looking for a one-and-done, I should probably go."

"What? Getting a virgin notch on your rock star belt isn't enough temptation for you?"

His brows furrow, and he sits back, pain written in his eyes. "Wow! Is that what you really think of me? You make me sound despicable."

I shrug, frowning. "Come on, don't act surprised. It's a well-known stereotype of bad-boy rockers."

"Maybe," he says, shaking his head. "But the fact you can't separate me as an individual from all bad-boy rocker stereotypes is a problem." He scratches his head, grimacing. "And here I thought you were finally starting to trust and like me for who I am rather than see me as some stupid generalization."

His phone rings again, and he looks angry enough to throw it through the living room window. "Motherfucker!" But then he looks at the caller ID, saying, "My phone's blowing up thanks to my bandmates. I better take this. I'm sorry." He lifts a finger to pause our conversation before answering.

I try hard not to listen to the one-sided talk, but it's almost impossible. "What? There's no way."

I don't know if I should stand up and leave the room. But I can't move from the couch, still caught up in a moment interrupted at the worst time possible.

"I don't believe you. I want proof." The rocker goes silent, shaking his head, his face livid. After a few moments, he says, "Proof of a positive test or a sonogram. Something more than just your word... Yeah, excuse me if I don't believe the shit that comes out of your mouth. Yeah, whatever..." His face hardens, and he says, "I want a paternity test as soon as that's possible. I'm not signing anything until then." He ends the call without saying goodbye, his face fuming.

I frown. Although I shouldn't jump to conclusions, I've heard enough to know what's happening. I wonder morosely if the conversation between my mom and Sax Gunner sounded much the same.

Rock buries his head in his hand for a long moment. The room feels thick with tension, pressed in and claustrophobic like it's closing in on us. "That was my ex, Lexie," he finally says, standing up and pacing before me. "She's been constant drama over the past two months. It never fucking ends. Now she's trying to say she's pregnant with my kid." He stops, looking at me with a somber face.

My brows knit, and the backs of my eyes sting. "Well, if she's two or more months along—"

He shakes his head, pacing some more. "No, there's no way. She's still drinking and partying... I can't tell you how many shots she pounded at a show we did in Orangevale the other night."

I press my lips firmly together, my heart breaking. "But it's a possibility, right?"

He crosses the room back and forth some more.

"It's always a possibility. But even if she is two months pregnant, God only knows how long she's been fucking around with Bub."

This is how deadbeat dads are born. I don't know what hurts worse. That I started letting my guard down with Rock tonight, or that he's looking more and more like my deadbeat father by the second. *Beware bad-boy rockers.*

"I need to go," he says quietly, looking at the wood floor. "I have a lot more phone calls to make."

I nod, a thousand emotions clobbering me over the head.

"The last thing I want to do is drag you into any of this," he observes, looking up timidly in my direction.

I keep my lips firmly pressed together rather than point out he already has. "I'm sorry about everything," I reply quietly, unsure what else to say. "Promise me you'll get to the bottom of what's happening before you make any big decisions."

The blood drains from his face, and he grimaces. "Maybe you're right about me. After all, this screams bad-boy rocker, doesn't it?" He paces back and forth some more, panic and realization setting in simultaneously. "Honestly, my gut tells me this is just another one of her attempts at stirring up drama. But, yes, I promise. Have a good night, Effie."

He grabs his jacket and hat as I follow him to the front door, standing in the entryway. Turning, he hugs me lightly. "You must think the worst of me."

I half smile, shaking my head because I can't speak. I don't want to jump to conclusions, but this hits way too close to home for me. "Merry Christmas, Rock—"

He nods curtly before trudging through the snow to his Bronco, a new weight on his shoulders I've never seen before.

Chapter Fourteen

EFFIE

I toss and turn for hours, unable to sleep. My mind races with the events of the evening and the myriad emotions they inspired. Emotions I still don't fully grasp. I close my eyes, remembering the duets from this evening and the brief make-out session.

Despite everything that transpired tonight with Lexie, I need Rock. *What does this mean?* I've heard more than once that women with daddy issues tend to gravitate toward men just like their dads.

Is that what's happening here?

I close my eyes, trying to sleep but surrendering to thoughts of Rock again. Dark, dirty thoughts. The kind that could get me in all sorts of trouble...

Would Rock thrill at how thoughts of him flood my pussy? Shiver at the sensation of my soft, melty folds enveloping his steel-straight rod? The thought of his sweaty flesh on mine, his hot breath on the crook of my neck and the shell of my ear. The way his voice would grumble and growl my name as ecstasy washed over his face...

Fantasies grip me, and tension builds, climbing to a

breaking point. I can't take it anymore. I've got to masturbate to relieve some of this longing. And to remind myself that I don't need Rock. Or any man, for that matter. I can take care of myself *in every way*.

In my nightstand drawer, I locate the cute little jar I keep filled with coconut oil for times like this. It's my favorite lube, soft, silky, and natural. But when house temperatures cool, it solidifies, which means breaking off a chunk that I warm in my hand.

Once the oil pools in my palm, I drip it over my pussy, using my oil-covered fingers to find my clit. I'm surprised by the already semi-swollen nub as I close my eyes, sighing long and hard. I need this release so badly that I throb from my fingers to my toes.

As I run my digits back and forth over my pearl, my pussy tightens, and my hips curl upwards, begging for the man I can't give them. I imagine the taste of Rock's generous, sensual lips as they graze over mine teasingly before his tongue dives into my mouth. I can only imagine what it would feel like buried in my pussy. I slide a finger inside my tight, wet channel, feeling the swell and flutter in my walls.

What I wouldn't give for this to be Rock's skilled fingers. I add a second, savoring the stretch and feeling of fullness. It's almost too much for me, but considering the cowboy's height and girth, I imagine he's much larger.

I fantasize about what his experienced hips would do as they glide over mine, finding the perfect rhythm and angle for deep, soul-shattering penetration. Taking me hard and hot, deflowering me with careless abandon until I skitter over the edge of pleasure and pain.

My breathing comes fast now as my mind continues wandering. The sensual sounds of our singing caress my ears, and in my mind's eye, I revisit his rugged, muscular back, covered in so many tattoos it's hard to know where one ends and the next begins.

Kind of like how I'd like him and I to be in our perfect dream world. So much a part of each other that people wouldn't know where the soul of one ends and the other begins. Kind of like how our voices melted into one another at the party, two halves of some greater whole that I didn't even know existed...until him.

Of course, none of this could ever happen in real life. But my heart clings savagely to the reverie.

I change the pace for a few swipes, slowing the strokes over my clit as I increase the pressure. I circle my nub slowly, my eyes rolling back in my head as I savor every sensation. Trying to replicate what Rock would experience if we were together like this.

His mouth greedily devouring my clit, making all sorts of wet, slurping sounds as he teases and explores me, flicking me with his teeth and swirling me on his hot, velvety tongue as his fingers demand everything from me.

I scream his name, grinding my pussy into his face and my fingernails into his rock-hard, tattoo-covered back. His thick, hard cock pulsing with greedy desire as he slams into me, again and again, claiming me with wanton desire...

My pussy gulps and milks my fingers as I scream into the empty air, "Rock!" Waves of pleasure wash over me, and my hand is wet with my arousal. It takes a few minutes for the tension to fully drain from my body and my breath to approach normalcy.

Rock could be sharing this bed with me right now, holding me against his firm, sweaty body as we catch our breaths together. But no, he's dealing with a situation that could change his life forever. I don't want to judge him or jump to conclusions, but I desperately hope he makes the right decision. *Please don't be like Sax was to me.*

The question, is what will that right decision look like? Taking Lexie back and trying to make things work? My stomach roils at the thought. Staying single and attempting to co-parent with a woman who sounds miserable to be tied to for eighteen years? The idea of her drinking while potentially pregnant upsets me the most. What kind of mother is she? Even mine didn't do that...

I don't understand enough about the situation to make any judgments. And I don't know Rock well enough to offer more than moral support and a person who will listen. If he decides to go the Sax route, though? Will I really be so good at listening?

That would be tough for me. Maybe impossible. A wound reopened tonight that's hard for me to describe, let alone process and deal with. And a large part of me, despite the inner warnings not to rush to conclusions, feels disgusted with myself for finding a man who's the antithesis of everything I believe in. And so very like my own father.

Beware bad-boy rock stars.

Is that really such hard advice to follow? Apparently, considering I just masturbated to fantasies of the guy after seriously considering giving my virginity to him. I don't know what Hollister's done to me, but this isn't good. Maybe I need to move back to Sacramento. Be done with this place.

But is it really my home, either? Especially with my mom head over heels for some new guy. Depending on what happens with their relationship, she may ignore me for months or even years. The woman is the epitome of codependent with men. Maybe there is no place for me. Maybe I'll be lonely forever.

Big, fat teardrops wet my face as the weight of complete and total loneliness catches up with me. Even worse than this feeling, though, is the stark realization that if I moved away from Hollister, I would miss Rock terribly. And his family, too. Despite all my disparaging thoughts, this place has grown on me and is starting to feel like my home.

This is why I didn't want to go to Rough & Ready Ranch for the holidays. Yes, I had many other excuses, but what I feared the most is falling in love with the place, Rock, and his family. Too late for that now.

Apart from the affection that's grown for this town and its inhabitants, I need to see what happens with our duets. I don't know what occurs between Rock and me every time we sing together, but I can't deny the magic. Nobody can.

My performances with him have been among the most satisfying of my musical journey, not that I've allowed myself to perform with many other people apart from Alex. But I can't deny the joy they bring me, even as they draw me into a dangerous circle of intimacy with the man I told myself I would never fall for.

Chapter Fifteen

ROCK

"Skates," I answer with a growl. I'm in my cramped studio at Wicked Skin, bent over a customer, finishing up a hyperrealistic gray and black back piece with skulls, bullets, and roses. This is my buddy Fierce Amestoy's third session, and I can tell by how he tenses every time the needle hits his skin that he's ready for a break. "Hold on a sec," I holler into the phone, sitting back on my stool.

"Mind if I take this, Bro?" I ask, waggling an eyebrow at Fierce.

"Totally fine." The burly-looking mountain man says, straightening up and cracking his back and neck. He shows himself outside while I pull off my black plastic gloves, throw them in the waste basket beside my station, and pick up the phone.

"What's up?" I grumble.

"No Happy New Year? You sound like the fucking Grinch or something. Bad night?"

"Yep," I say, pressing my lips firmly together. The world could end, and Skates would be the last person I confide in.

"Back to the bottle so soon?" He says it with a laugh that

makes me wonder how sincere his support over the last few months has been.

"Nope, girl trouble. Nothing new." The drama with Lexie has monopolized the past week, leaving little room for me to even think about what went down with Effie on Christmas Eve. As much as I want her, I don't want to drag her into my current situation, especially when I still have so few answers about whether Lexie's claims are true. On top of that, Effie's comment about a virgin notch on my belt hurt my feelings. There's no other way to put it.

"Speaking of girls. Who the hell's the female singer on those tracks?"

I clear my throat, feeling my heart race in anticipation of saying her name. It's pathetic. "Josephine Jackson."

"Never heard of her."

I hesitate for a moment. Should I tell Skates that Effie is the daughter of Sax Gunner? As much as it might make him sweeten the deal, it's not my story to tell. Instead, I say, "There's no reason you should know her apart from the fact she's got a fan-fucking-tastic voice."

"You've got that right."

"So, you see potential there?"

"Fuck, yeah. Of course, I need to see what it's like working with you both in the studio. But I would definitely be open to a collaboration. And I bet with a solid demo tape to send out, we could get you two something solid."

"What do you mean by something solid?"

"Something game-changing."

I exhale slowly. "Something without the Lowlifes?"

"If I'm speaking out of turn, let me know. But I figure that's what you're after, the way the whole Lexie thing went down..."

"Went down? It's still fucking going down. Now, she's got Bub in a tizzy, convinced she's pregnant with my kid. But I have yet to see one shred of evidence of this. No sonogram, no proof of a positive pregnancy test. Hell, she can't give me a straight answer on a due date or when her next OBGYN appointment is."

"She really is next-level, isn't she?"

I agree, "Anymore she is. She fucked up cheating on me. That's the bottom line. And I'm over it and her. She doesn't seem to get that, though. And Bub isn't helping things, either. It's going to be the end of the band." I straighten my shoulders, stretching my back and neck. Tattooing is hard on posture, especially with how I've hunched over Fierce for hours now.

"So, Lexie's your Yoko Ono?"

"More like our Paul McCartney after Brian Epstein," I retort.

He chuckles. "Maybe this is all for the best. Just between you and me, the Lowlifes have been holding you back. I could take you so much further without them." If I had a quarter every time a music producer blew smoke up my ass like this, I'd have a two-story, forty-eight-hundred square foot tattoo parlor.

"Honestly, I don't know how much further I want to go. I'm happy with my tattoo parlor and my real estate acquisitions in Hollister. I'm sitting pretty at the moment and kind of like it. You know, the musician lifestyle has a way of dragging you down over time. Constantly traveling...living on buses between stops, subsisting on shitty-ass roadside food. It's a heart attack in the making. And all to serenade a bunch of spoiled rotten brats who spit their gum at me while I sing."

He laughs nervously, knowing negotiations have begun. "Well, you don't go into the punk or rockabilly scene for respect. Look how fans treat Mike Ness from Social D."

"God help me if I'm still touring at Mike Ness's age. Fucking pathetic." A twinge of guilt seizes me because I love his music. But for heaven's sake. The guy's old enough to be my grandfather.

"Speaking of old rockers, I tracked down Sax Gunner for you. His personal number and everything. I also relayed a message through his manager that you'll be in touch, and Sax said he was looking forward to it. Apparently, you've made a good impression on him in the past. I'll email his contact info over after this call."

"Much appreciated." After the way things ended with Effie the other night, I feel ambivalent about this whole subject. But then again, maybe if she has some closure in this area of her life, she'll be more open to a professional relationship with me...and maybe more. Of course, all bets could be off, depending on what happens with Lexie.

"Now, back to getting you and the girl some exposure. What do you want to make this happen? Because I need this duo. I mean, you need this duo."

My ears perk up. It's not often Skates gets interested enough for a Freudian slip. I yawn, shaking my head. "Well, I'm also only one half of the equation, and although Josephine and I fit together on musical terms, I'm not sure she's on board with much else about me."

"Shit," he says with a dark laugh. "Do I need to have the same talk with you I had with Bub. Music is business, not pleasure. Keep your dick in your pants for once and think with your big boy brain."

I'm developing a complex between Effie's declaration the other night and now Skates's. That said, I definitely made the rounds over the years. As the lead singer of a decently popular rockabilly band, pussy was something I never ran out of. Makes me wonder why I can't just move past Effie now. She said it herself. Why settle for her when I can have my pick? Because she's like no woman I've ever met before, which makes the fallout at her house a week ago all the more painful.

"Surprisingly, she doesn't hate me because we slept together. She more detests me as a general rule."

"Great, then you'll be the next incarnation of the Civil Wars." Skates clearly doesn't want to take "no" for an answer. "Only the Wanda Jackson and Elvis Presley version."

I can't deny hearing our voices together for the first time made me think of the Civil Wars, too. And ironically enough, their hatred of each other outside of the studio is so fucking legendary documentaries have been made about it. Sure, that kind of epic tension sells albums. But the thought of Effie and I settling into a hate-filled stalemate behind the scenes while making the musical equivalent of love on stage night after night makes my heart ache. I absent-mindedly rub the spot over my chest, exhaling loudly.

"Rock? You still there?"

"Yeah, man. Just thinking everything through..."

Chapter Sixteen

ROCK

F ierce bursts back into my studio, blood and ink glistening from the newest portions of his ink. I motion silently for him to sit while I grab the phone, speaking into it. "Time's up, Skates. Let me mull this over, and I'll be in touch."

Not only do I have to mull it over, I have to break the news to Effie. I have no clue how she'll react.

"Wait a second, man. I thought you were asking me for a favor. What the fuck is this?" A thin slice of fury pierces his otherwise jovial voice.

"Buddy, I'm in the middle of a tattoo right now. So, let me call you back. Okay?"

"Alright," he growls testily, ending the call.

"Who's that?" Fierce asks, raising his brow.

I shake my head. "My producer. It can fucking wait."

"What can wait?"

I level my gaze on my friend, tempted for a moment to explain to him what happened. But this is a tiny fucking town, and gossip flies faster than a swallow. Besides, Fierce's family, the Amestoys, have a longstanding beef with mine. As I understand it, he and Christian were even in a fistfight a couple years back, which I would have given my right hand to see. Apparently, Fierce beat the shit out of my brother.

As much as I love Christian, he's lorded his role as an older brother over us our whole lives. Seeing him on the receiving end of a good licking would be fucking fantastic, especially with a cold brew in my hand and a lawn chair. Fantasies aside, I wouldn't trust an Amestoy as far as I could throw one, and at two hundred or more pounds, I doubt old Fierce would see much air time. So, I deflect, saying, "Talking music shop. Besides, what you told me a few minutes ago is way more interesting. What's that matching site called again?"

He twists back into position as I slap on a new set of disposable gloves and wipe away the ink and blood weeping from his design. He grimaces slightly, and I'd wager he doesn't have more than a half-hour left in him. For as big and muscular as the former high school linebacker is, he's a real pussy when it comes to pain. But he's also a well-paying regular, so I keep this to myself.

"Mountain Mates," he says with a growl as the needle hits his livid skin again.

"My brother, Ridge, could use something like that if it's what it sounds like..."

Fierce grunts, his face twisting with pain. "It's for mountain men looking for women, kind of like Farmer Wants a Wife. No offense, Ridge is probably too wild even for that shit."

"Don't I know it," I laugh. "Have you heard Ridge has been making survivalist videos and posting them on YouTube and TikTok? Apparently, some are blowing up pretty good."

Fierce laughs, an anguished edge to his voice. "I guess some people are into the whole semi-evolved caveman vibe."

I pause, reading my client's tortured expression. "If we need to stop early, man. That's fine."

"Are you fucking kidding me? No, I'm finishing this today...no matter what. Besides, you have a year and a half waiting list for tattoo clients."

"Yeah, I'm pretty damn booked up into the foreseeable future. But for you, I'd make an exception. And you figure someone's going to cancel."

"Maybe," he grunts as I grind the needle into his flesh to get the desired shadows. "God, you have a heavy hand sometimes," he grumbles.

"You want it to look good or not?"

"Yeah, I do," he says, tensing his body and resigning himself to take the punishment. "I want this done before Felicity shows up."

"Felicity? You mean the chick you've been talking to on that app? Are you seriously considering marrying a woman sight unseen?"

"Well, I have a ton of her photos, and we FaceTime almost daily. So, it's not like I don't know what she looks like—"

"Yeah, but dude, marriage is forever." He shrugs, and I let out a tense tsk. "What did I tell you about moving, brah? You want a shitty-ass tattoo or what?"

He doesn't reply. Instead, he answers by gritting his teeth so hard that I can see the muscle jumping beneath his beard and hear his enamel screaming.

"What if she's catfishing you and a five-hundred-pound Sumo wrestler shows up or something? You still going to go through with it?"

He chuckles almost imperceptibly, and I can tell he's focusing on not moving an inch. I take my hint, going back to concentrating on my lines and shading. The last thing he needs as he tries to grit this out is me busting his balls.

But the thought of him marrying someone he barely knows is mind-boggling. He's told me it's either that or his dad's arranging for a bride from the Basque Country. Still, I don't understand why a guy of his size and power would relinquish his fate to anyone else.

Maybe he's on to something, though. It's not like my current trajectory is getting me any closer to a meaningful relationship I can count on. In fact, the latest debacle has me so turned around and confused that I don't know which end is up when it comes to women and dating.

Contrary to my earlier predictions, Fierce holds out. When I make the final sweep over his flesh before announcing I'm finished, he lets out a long, pained sigh. "Thank fuck. That took me way to my edge, Bro."

I wipe his back, reviewing care instructions, which he's heard too many times to count. "You've got Aquaphor handy?"

"Of course."

"And you remember that even though I'll wrap it with Saran Wrap here, get that shit off within the first twenty-four hours."

"Yada yada yada... Don't scratch it. Wash it, but don't scrub it in the shower... I get it." I hand him a mirror, which he angles to look at the piece from the mirrored wall of my studio. "That's fucking amazing."

"It did come out nice, didn't it?" I reply, ready to go home, relax, and drink a cold soda. It's long days like this that nearly tempt me back into alcohol. I could seriously use a long neck.

"By the time your girl gets here, it should be healed up perfectly. So don't worry about her putting a few claw marks in it," I say with a wink, bringing my fist up to bump his. For the first time in his life, Fierce hesitates at my suggestive words, looking a bit conflicted.

"No offense, man. But could you lay off talking about my old lady that way?"

I raise my eyebrows with a laugh as I work on wrapping his back. "Yeah, no problem, man. I'm happy for you."

"Thanks," he says with a nod, digging into his back pocket and pulling out a wad of money he hands me. "That should do it with tip."

I nod.

"You want to count it?"

I chuckle. "Nah, I know you're good for it. And if I find you shorted me, I'll send Christian over to collect."

The big Basque man laughs. "Yeah, you do that." He stomps out, looking and moving like he's pissed off. It's his normal mood, as far as I can tell.

Coolie sits at the reception desk in front of the computer where we schedule appointments. "That piece is wicked, Dog. I hope you got plenty of pictures."

"Sure did. I'm going to clean up and head out." Looking outside, I'm surprised to see it's already inky black. Glancing at the clock, I realize how much time has flown by. "Already after seven?" That's crazy.

Coolie doesn't move an inch, which makes me curious. "Aren't you out of here for the night?"

"Nah, Bro. I got one more appointment."

My eyes narrow. He knows I'm not a big fan of late-night appointments, as that's when most of the trouble happens. "Who are you tattooing so late?"

He shrugs. "One of my regulars. She wanted in before Christmas, but this is the soonest I could do. It won't take long. Just a quickie."

"Sure," I laugh. "No sex in the parlor. It's highly unprofessional, and the last thing I need the health department catching wind of."

"What's the fun in that?"

"It's called being a business owner," I grumble. "Move the fuck over. He stands up slowly, heading back towards his studio, and I start to close out his calendar when my eyes fixate on a name: Effie Jackson.

Chapter Seventeen

EFFIE

I lie on the floor, breathing deeply and surrendering to savasana. Part of turning over a new leaf, I chose yoga over cheap champagne and a hangover this New Year's Day, and the internal glow and deep relaxation I feel confirm I made the right decision.

Suddenly, the phone rings, and I sit up on my yoga mat. At first, I decide not to answer the phone. After all, Mom is off gallivanting with a new beau, my new friends are all busy with family functions, and I haven't heard from Rock since Christmas Eve. I don't know what I was expecting. It's not like we spent time on the phone before that, and with the whole Lexie situation, I imagine he's swamped. Still, the way we left things was truly dissatisfying and left plenty of painful unanswered questions.

Maybe it's a telemarketer.

But then I relent after the fourth ring on the off-chance it could be my Lazarus. Answering the phone, I hear Mom exclaim, "Effie!" She bursts into tears, and I have to pull my ear away from the phone because it's so loud.

"What's wrong?" I ask, my heart jumping into my throat as I fear some kind of tragedy or death in the family.

"Fred left me," she balls.

"Fred? Who the heck is Fred?" I ask, shaking my head and feeling my stomach drop.

"The man I spent Christmas with."

Maybe if I hadn't spent the past week reading up on narcissistic parents and journaling, I could hold my tongue. But not anymore. Instead, I state, "I thought you were so busy working over Christmas that you couldn't hang out with me."

"Oh, well, that, too."

"You lied to me, Mom."

Mom sobs inconsolably. "Effie, you're seriously going to guilt trip me on top of what I'm going through with Fred?" She asks the question but doesn't wait for an answer. I realize she doesn't need an answer because everything is always, utterly, and entirely about her and her alone. As if confirming this, she continues, "I found these texts in his phone...of him sexting his ex-wife, and when I confronted him, he left."

"Good riddance," I say, rubbing my temples and trying to understand the problem.

"But I thought he was the one, Effie. Now, what am I going to do?"

"I don't know. Get back on Tinder?" The woman goes through men faster than a robin through earthworms on a rainy day. If falling in love could be declared a world record, she would hold titles for rapidity and number of repetitions.

I could tell her all of this, and I have half a mind to. But I also know it will change nothing.

Still, loneliness makes me stay on the phone longer than I should. After all, she's the only person I'll likely speak to today apart from Coolie at Wicked Skin. My pulse races at the thought of being in Rock's tattoo shop. Not that I'll see the inked cowboy, but the hope remains. "I'm sorry, Mom. Tell me everything that happened." I roll my eyes, settling in for a lengthy conversation. At least she's finally talking to me and noticing me again...even if she missed her promise to call me on Christmas Day by nearly a week.

An hour later, she laughs and jokes with me. We've scrutinized everything that happened in her brief "relationship" from every angle, and I've finally nudged her into going out for a girls' night to gain a newfound perspective. Again.

"Besides, there's always a good chance I'll accidentally bump into Fred, and then he'll see how amazing I look and totally regret what he did. Maybe if I'm lucky, he'll even grovel." There goes sixty minutes of coaching her through her breakup.

Thank God I'm not FaceTiming her, as I can't contain the expressions washing over my face. I have no words, waiting awkwardly for her to say something else.

"But enough about me. Tell me how your holidays went. By the way, I missed you too much, baby girl. Don't ever make me do another holiday season without you."

"But Mom, you're the one who canceled on me."

"Really, Effie? How long are you going to hold a grudge?"

I sigh, biting my tongue. The kittens bound into my lap, and I reach for one, sinking a hand into its soft fur as I talk. Suddenly, it latches onto my hand with its claws and teeth, attacking me unprovoked. "Ouch! Stop it, you little brat!" I cry.

"Who are you talking to?" Mom asks.

"One of the kittens I'm fostering."

"But didn't you tell me your hot tattooed cowboy landlord has a strict no-pets policy? Maybe I need to come visit you and check this guy out for myself."

It's far from the first time Mom has tried to come after a guy I liked. Hell, she famously stole my high school sweetheart, who I thought was my soulmate and the love of my life, when she was going through one of her many midlife crises. The memory still gives me a monster case of heartburn.

"But he's a bad-boy rocker. Didn't you always warn me to stay away from them?"

She chuckles. "Oh, honey, you've always been a rule follower." She says it dismissively, making my head spin.

"I grew up on a constant diet of how Sax Gunner destroyed your life by getting you pregnant. Getting saddled with me was why you couldn't pursue the career you wanted, get a good man, or enjoy the life you always dreamed of living. Is that not what you always told me. Beware of bad-boy rockers?"

"Well, sweetie. For you, I would say that the advice holds true. Except you and I both know you're more likely to end up a lonely, single cat lady."

Rock could not have been more right about this woman's narcissism. "Lonely, single, cat lady. Ouch!"

"Well, how did you spend the holidays?" Before I can breathe, let alone answer, she finishes, "My point exactly."

Maybe something got knocked loose the night Rock left unexpectedly. Perhaps the last week of self-reflection has done it. But I'm seriously done with this conversation. And for the first time in my life, I'm also done with my mother's selfishness, immaturity, and demeaning comments.

"Okay, hold it right there. I just spent the last sixty minutes listening to you complain about Fred and the failed relationship that kept you from spending Christmas with your only daughter. And now, you're going to turn around and berate me for spending Christmas alone? Even though, if you'd stop long enough to listen to anything I had to say, you would know that I attended a party and had an amazing time."

"It always has to be about you, doesn't it, Effie?"

Oh my God! This woman. Now that I know what to look for, I see things more clearly. As painful as it is, recognizing the toxicity for what it is provides an escape route. One free of the guilt and shame she employed in the past to control me. "Look, you have a girls' night to get to, and I have to get ready for my next tattoo. As fun and enlightening as this conversation has been, all I can say is good luck, and I hope you find what you're looking for."

She talks as if I haven't said a thing, and I finally have to cut her off, saying, "I have to go now. Have a great night."

I sit on the floor a long time, the kitties skittering over my lap, staring at the wall. Despite feeling empowered by the boundaries I set in this conversation and keeping the conversation to an hour rather than two or more, I feel exhausted. Still, excitement brews as I look down at my phone, seeing it's one o'clock, giving me just enough time to prepare for my appointment.

Pushing the kittens gently out of my lap, I bustle around my bedroom, getting ready to shower, when my cell phone buzzes. *Please don't let it be Mom again.*

Grabbing it, I see a text from Coolie:

> Mind if we move the appointment to 8? I'm a little behind.

Eight on New Year's Day feels odd to me, but I really want my next tattoo, and even more than that, I want to see Rock.

I text back:

> That works for me. See you then!

The appointment time change allows me to take a long shower and set my hair in rollers. Soon, I find myself doing a DIY manicure and pedicure and full makeup with black cat eyeliner. Between that and the Marilyn Monroe do, I decide to go all out, wearing a girdle that cinches my waist, a pair of silky black stockings with lines up the back, and an adorable black

1950s-style black pencil skirt with a white silky top that ties at the neck and flutters at my shoulders.

It's sexy without showing my cleavage and totally my style. Coupled with a pair of black heels that are anything but snow- and ice-ready and a leopard-spotted swing coat, I leave for my appointment fully prepared to stun Rock...if he's there.

Please, please, please let him be there.

I drive carefully, mindful of black ice, although the last two days have been unseasonably warm and gone a long way toward melting the accumulation from Christmas Day. Parking in front of the shop like I always do, I pick my way carefully along the pavement so I don't fall flat on my face in my heels. I look for Rock's Bronco but don't see it. Of course, if he parked behind the shop, I won't be able to see it, and I don't feel like poking around the back in the dark. In fact, I make a mental note never to have an appointment this late again, as it's kind of spooky out here.

Entering the shop, Coolie greets me, seated in the chair behind the computer where he makes appointments. "Hot damn!" he exclaims, letting his eyes rove over me. "You look good enough to eat."

My face flushes. Although I'm used to Coolie flirting with me, I feel a little self-conscious with how over the top I've gone. The lateness of the evening and the fact the shop seems deadly quiet also makes me feel more nervous than usual.

"Are we still thinking roses on your calf?" he asks, and I nod.

Clearing his throat, he says, "Because your thigh might be a better fit. Give me more space to work." He licks his lips, eyeing me greedily. My stomach churns, and I'm ready to turn around and march right back out of the shop.

But noise and bustling from one of the back rooms grab my attention. We both turn our heads towards the sounds at the same time.

Suddenly, Rock saunters into the reception area, taking one look at me and going beet red. His face looks deadly somber, and he doesn't try to hide the way his gaze devours me. His eyes blacken, and his brows furrow. He looks at Coolie for a moment and then back at me, declaring in a raw voice, "What the fuck are you waiting for, Coolie? You can go home now. This one's mine."

I inhale sharply, my cheeks burning.

"Nah, dog, you can't go stealing one of my regular clients," Coolie protests. But the tattooed cowboy gives him a look so fierce that Coolie shrugs, adding, "Alright, man. Whatever. But does the lady even want you to tattoo her?"

Both men look at me, and I feel like a deer in headlights. I open my mouth, but no words come out.

"She's mine," Rock growls.

"No, last time I checked, she's my fucking client. This is her second appointment. Isn't it, darling?" Coolie directs the last question to me.

Rock interjects, "Don't ever call her 'darling' again. Now, I don't know if you're stupid or stubborn, so let me make this clear to you. The next man who lays a hand on this woman fucking dies. Make sure Muffin gets the memo, too. You understand, asshole? Now, why don't you get the hell out of here before I decide to quit being nice."

Coolie stands, frowning and glaring hard at Rock. Sauntering towards him, he comes within inches of bumping his chest, trying to get in his face. But he's a good five to six inches shorter and not remotely built like the muscular tattoo shop owner who easily holds his ground. "We're good enough to run your shop when you're off gallivanting. But then you return and poach our clients? When you've got a fucking eighteen-month waiting list? This is fucking bullshit."

"And what are you going to do about it?" Rock grumbles

so low it's almost inaudible, his eyes narrowing, his body taut like a panther ready to pounce.

Coolie stops, assessing the situation for a moment before stepping back. He looks like a defeated man trying to play it off as though he doesn't care when he clearly does. Rock looks livid. I half expect steam to come out of his ears.

The aggressive way the inked cowboy eyes me makes my body burn and my mind race. I open my mouth to excuse myself home, unprepared to take the brunt of whatever anger rages in the man after this crazy scene. But I can't find words.

"You done, motherfucker?" Rock says in a near whisper, and Coolie nods, looking away and hunching his shoulders. The cowboy watches as Coolie collects his stuff and walks out, his movements hurried though he tries to play it cool. After the shorter man leaves, Rock locks the front door, making my heart race. Nodding down the long hallway towards the studios, he barks, "This way."

I hesitate for a moment before following him, anxious like a middle schooler headed to the principal's office for a stern talking to. The air feels thick, and I have trouble breathing. He directs me into a small room lined with stunning artwork. Despite the tension in the air, I ask breathlessly, looking at the walls, "Are these all yours?"

He nods, his frown deepening. He motions toward his black leather reclining tattoo chair, and I scramble into the seat, turning to look at him. His face glows dangerous and wrath-filled as he sits on his rolling stool.

Chapter Eighteen

EFFIE

The muscle in Rock's jaw jumps as he clenches his teeth, and he says in dark tones, "So, you made an appointment for eight at night on New Year's Day with Coolie to get roses tattooed on your calf? And then he tried to talk you into a thigh tattoo?"

"Yes," I stammer, watching the cowboy devolve into simmering fury. "But I would never agree to the thigh."

His face is grim, his eyes narrow, and his lips pressed into a thin line.

"You threatened to kill Coolie if he touched me again," My voice shakes, and my brows knit. "What is going on?"

"You judge me by stereotypes. Last time I saw you, you told me I was a fucking bad-boy rock star who wanted a virgin notch in his belt. Remember that shit? Well, what do you think the stereotype is of a girl who shows up at a tattoo parlor at eight at night dressed like you? Coolie had one thing on his mind. It wasn't ink."

"Coolie's always been nice and respectful to me—"

"You're so fucking innocent sometimes. You're going to get yourself in serious trouble, the kind you can't get out of.

Besides, I don't need you creating drama between me and my employees. I mean, look what just happened between Coolie and me on account of you."

"Are you blaming me?" I ask, blinking a few times hard.

"Yes, because he and I got along fine before I saw your name on the schedule. Now, I'm ready to kill the mother-fucker... Lord knows I've already dealt with enough drama from my ex-girlfriend, Lexie."

I don't know if I should ask or even want the answer, but curiosity grips me. "Have you heard anything else about the situation with your ex?"

He sighs, looking exhausted. "I've seen no proof because I'm ninety-nine percent sure there is none. But she's still milking it for everything it's worth. And because Bub's an idiot when it comes to women, it's ripping the Lowlifes apart."

"I'm sorry to hear that," I say quietly.

"Good riddance," he replies caustically. "You must fucking hate me under the circumstances." He side-eyes me coolly. "I've fulfilled all your bad-boy rocker stereotypes, haven't I? I'm surprised you're even giving me the time of day right now."

My face burns as I shake my head. "This could happen to anyone... The question is, what will you do if she's telling the truth?" I swallow hard, my heart pounding inside my chest. Only now do I realize how much I need this answer.

"I'll stick by the baby. It won't be his or her fault. But as for Lexie? I want nothing to do with her. She's trouble. More than you can fucking imagine."

I nod. "Thank you."

"Why are you thanking me? This has nothing to do with you."

I raise my chin defiantly. "It's about doing the right thing.

And your answer tells me a lot about what kind of man you are."

"No child should have to suffer for the inadequacies of his or her parents, although it happens all the time. Doesn't it, Blackbird?"

"More than it should."

We stare awkwardly at each other for a long moment. Rock's eyes rove over me, a mixture of anger and tenderness. "Now that I've answered your question, will you answer mine?"

I nod.

"Why in the hell are you dressed to the nines like a rocka-billy pinup girl for a late-night tattoo appointment with Coolie?"

"Pinup girl? Rock, this is how I dress when I want to look nice." *I'm not even showing cleavage.*

"That's the problem! Why in the fuck do you want to look nice for Coolie?" His face flushes crimson, and he looks like he's about to put his fist through the wall. His eyes settle on my legs, and he adds furiously, "Goddammit, Josephine! You have fucking seamed stockings on."

"And so?" I bluster, knitting my brows. "I don't own any other types of stockings."

"Fuck!" Rock exclaims, looking up at the ceiling and fuming. His adult-male tantrum reminds me more of one of my kinder-gartners than he probably wants to hear. Instead of acknowl-edging this, I give him a moment to collect his emotions, studying the inked cowboy and trying to figure him out. His jealousy is overwhelming. But instead of it scaring or repelling me, I like the reassurance that comes with it. He wants me like I want him.

Rock wears a black and white Bad Religion T-shirt with an unbuttoned red and black flannel shirt, black Dickies, a brown Carhartt beanie, and steel-toed combat boots. He's got a chain running from the wallet in his back pocket to his belt loop like he's working overtime to bring the Grungie early two thousands back. I love the cool, nostalgic vibe.

"Answer my question. Why in the fuck are you this dressed up for a tattoo from Coolie?"

How he looks at me leaves no room for half-truths.

I confess tentatively, "I was hoping to see you again."

He exhales sharply, glaring a hole through me.

"I made the appointment before Christmas when you and I barely talked. Kind of like now," I reply, arching my eyebrow with my last statement. "And then Coolie texted this afternoon asking me to move my three o'clock appointment to later. With all the extra time and nowhere else to be today, I decided to dress up. You know, in case our paths crossed again."

"I'm not buying this. No fucking way. You've never dressed up like this for me before."

His words make me sit back, my heart pounding. My tongue darts out to wet my bottom lip, and I purse my mouth, looking at him long and hard. The flush of his reddened cheeks, his searing turquoise eyes, how his nostrils flare, and the way his jaw muscle bulges. The man is stark, raving jealous, and I love it. Going a week without hearing from him made me question his feelings for me, but this display couldn't be more obvious.

I observe in measured tones, "I've never had the chance to prepare before seeing you. You always kind of show up when least expected."

He nods jerkily, looking at his black combat boots.

Steeling my voice, I ask, "Aren't you listening to what I'm telling you? I dressed up this way for you, Rock. Because I was hoping I might see you again during my appointment. After how things ended at my place and the rude things I said before you got the news. When you didn't talk to me for a week, I wondered what was happening."

"I didn't know what to tell you, and I didn't want to drag you into my drama. You deserve better than that." His eyes narrow as he dissects me. "But I don't get it. If you wanted to see me, why didn't you call, text, or make an appointment with me?"

I sit up, turning in the chair so that I'm no longer reclining, and my toes point towards him, my legs dangling over the side. I keep my knees firmly pressed together in the ladylike way my grandmother taught me. God only knows what my mother would be doing in this exact scenario. "The first time I ever called Wicked Skin, Muffin and Coolie told me you're booked out for more than a year. And you just reconfirmed that."

"God, Effie, don't even say those guys' names around me. The thought of them touching you. Of them marking your skin," he growls.

My eyes round, and I stare blankly at him, unsure what to say.

The corners of his mouth turn down slightly, and he grimaces. Removing his beanie and running his hand through his chestnut-colored hair, he concedes with a growl, "Between touring with the Lowlifes and the fact people come from all over the United States for one of my portraits, you're looking at a long line."

I nod, scanning the room and the skilled drawings on the wall again. He specializes in black and gray, hyperrealistic portraits like Kat Von D. The faces I see are stunning and lifelike.

Turning my gaze back on my Lazarus, he looks tortured beneath my gaze. "What the fuck am I going to do with you?" he whispers, frustration laced in his voice as he puts his beanie back on. I can't tell if he's asking me this question or talking to himself.

Chapter Nineteen

EFFIE

"Maybe we should see more of each other," I say softly, my eyes roaming over his handsome face. I forgot how gorgeous he is with his straight, proportionate nose, his square-cut jawline, and the perfect brow for unending James Dean scowls. "We still have a lot to learn about each other."

"Is that what you really want? I thought that with the news from Lexie, you'd want nothing to do with me. Even though I still think it's total bullshit."

I shake my head. "No, I just needed the reassurance you would do the right thing."

"And would you do it with me if I asked?" He raises a questioning eyebrow. "Ride or die?"

My breath catches in my throat, and my heart expands. In a shaky voice, I admit something I've known since Christmas Eve that still scares and thrills me in equal measures. "There's still a lot to figure out between us. But if things keep going the way they have since we started singing together? Yes, Rock, I would without hesitation."

Emotion clouds his eyes, and he stares at me more

tenderly, the shields he's raised dropping one by one. "So, you dress like this often?" he asks gruffly.

I nod. "I do when I have someone I'm trying to look good for."

"And you swear to God that this is for me and not Coolie?" Rock asks, eyeing me wildly. "Because I can't fuck around like this and keep my sanity. You know the havoc Lexie has wreaked with the Lowlifes. It's part of how I ended up in your bushes back in October. I don't do well with stuff like this, and Lexie never made me feel even half of what I do…"

I raise my brows as his voice trails off, willing him to finish his thought.

He shakes his head, looking defeated. "For you, Effie. So, if you ever fuck me over, I don't know what I'll do. Or if I'll even survive it." Despite the melodramatic nature of his words, one look at his somber face tells me he speaks sincerely. He continues, "I know that sounds fucking stupid because we barely know each other, but when we sing together, it's like I've found the missing part of me. And I don't want any other man putting his grubby hands on that… *on you*." Rock's face is animated with jealousy as he talks, and he uses his hands, drawing my eyes to the tattooed letters on his fingers.

"What do those stand for?" I ask quietly, not meaning to change the subject but intensely curious to know everything about this man I'm not supposed to like but feel myself falling for. I point to the space on his fingers between the first and second knuckles.

He folds his hands together, letting his fingers face me so that I read "Sick Boy" with a dancing skeleton on his pinkie.

A broad smile captures my lips. "Social D. I love that band."

"Sick boy, sick girl. That could be you and me, you know," he says, grabbing my hands in my lap and squeezing them.

Electricity shuttles between our flesh, making my cheeks flush and a knot grow in my throat that I have trouble swallowing.

"It could, couldn't it? And your hair, Rock. I've been meaning to ask you how you do it when you're not wearing a hat. If you do it at all?"

He leans down, kissing my folded hands, his face and lips so close to my pussy I can barely breathe. He has to know he's being naughty, yet he plays it off like it's the most natural thing. But then he looks up, his dark, devil-may-care face so over-the-top sexy, I swear I lose my virginity right there, and my ovaries explode for good measure.

"You have to come to one of the Lowlife shows. I grease it rockabilly style, although, on some occasions, I do the hawk instead."

My hands find his face, palming his rough cheeks peppered in afternoon stubble and wondering what's gotten into me. All I know is his face feels good in my hands, better than good. Like I was made to touch this man. "That's super hot, Rockwell Landry."

He grins, his hands sliding to my hips on either side, his fingertips squeezing and caressing the curve down to my legs. "You're the only person on the face of this Earth who calls me by my full legal name. Well, you and my dad sometimes. But that's only when he's pissed at me."

"It's a nice name. I like it."

"Everybody else thinks it's a dumbass name."

I shake my head, enjoying the caress of my fingers over his rugged jawline and unshaven cheeks more than I care to admit. "It is an old person's name. I'll give you that. When we corresponded by email before I moved in, I envisioned you as this eighty-year-old retired professor or something. With your own garden filled with gnomes."

"Sorry to disappoint." He chuckles darkly, turning his head

sideways in my lap as I stroke his cheek some more. If I didn't know better, I'd think the man was about to start purring. His fingers continue to tease and trace the curves of my hips with circular motions that grow larger and cover more of my ass with each pass.

Even more alluring is the hot spot on my skirt above my pussy, warmed by his breath, which has my panties dripping. I'm ashamed to stand up from the tattoo chair with the uncustomary way my body responds to him. I can't imagine anything more embarrassing than leaving a wet spot behind.

"Keep those creepy ass garden gnomes away from me. You don't know what it was like waking up to an angel singing, speared on a thorn bush with those little guys staring me down O.K. Corral style. I couldn't tell if I died and went to heaven, or I was waiting in hell to have demons pick my bones dry. With how I lived my life up to that point, the second option made much more sense."

I chuckle, my voice growing silkier and darker as his big hands cover my ass and hips, squeezing and massaging me. "What are we doing, Rock?" I ask breathlessly, feeling the juncture between my legs throb painfully.

"What we were made to do," he replies in deep, resonant tones.

"Like on the Discovery Channel?" I tease.

"No, I'm not talking Nine Inch Nails, Blackbird. I mean, like you and I made for each other. It's torture to be away from you, Josephine, although I don't honestly claim to understand how you feel about me. But for me, this week has been hell without seeing you."

"For me, too," I whisper my whole body on fire with yearning.

He leans into me now, kissing the spot on my skirt over my pussy and making no compunctions about the dirty move. He buries his face in my skirt, taking a deep breath and looking at me punch-drunk. "I love how you smell," he says slowly and sensually.

My breath catches in my throat, and my hand goes to my chest. I don't mean to clutch my pearls, but this is a lot for a virgin who considered herself not interested in relationships not so long ago. I'm ready to spread my legs and beg him to work his magic.

Wrapping his hands around my waist and pulling me closer, he keeps his head in my lap, saying darkly, "For the record, I'd prefer if you weren't a virgin because I don't want to hurt you...ever. But the thought of any other man touching you. Fuck, I can't deal with that shit, either. You have to promise to forgive me when the time comes."

Rock and I are talking about having sex as though it's an inevitability. Instead of laughing nervously or putting him in his place as I would any other guy on the planet, I blush, saying tenderly, "Of course."

He smiles, reveling in our intimacy like a cat stretched out in the sun. I remove his beanie clumsily, my hands shaky with want, tangling my fingers in his thick, soft hair. Bending forward, I kiss his temple and then his rough cheek. All I know is I've never felt more loved or wanted by another human being, and I don't want it to end. *Ever.*

"You have to promise to forgive me whenever I'm unlovable or stupid. And I swear to do the same with you. Can you handle that?" he adds, scowling at me in that *Rebel Without a Cause* way that makes me want to jump his bones.

My eyes round, and I say without thinking, "Not if it involves other women. I could never put up with that." I press my lips firmly together at the end for emphasis.

"So, you do feel about me the way I feel about you," he observes, stealing another happy glance at me as he kisses the same spot on my skirt for a second time, lingering longer. My lower core is a tight jumble of tension, and I feel like I could explode. Even scarier, I'm no longer thinking straight at all. It's as if the man has somehow short-circuited my brain.

"Yes," I whisper, and he pulls me closer to him, possessively holding my hips and ass. I stroke his hair like he's my pet, still leaning down intermittently to kiss him until I've covered nearly every square inch of his face but his lips. I even kiss his eyelid, the tip of his nose, and his earlobe, which makes him laugh.

"Then, why'd you say those things to me on Christmas Eve?" Rock asks, eyeing me with morose curiosity. My hands stop in his hair, and I look at him long and hard, weighing if I should tell him the unadulterated truth.

Seeing where the blatant truth-telling approach has gotten me so far, I decide to continue, even though the backs of my eyes sting, and I struggle to find the right words. "Because I felt insanely vulnerable in front of you, and I was trying to protect myself. Put up my shields."

"I don't want you to feel like you have to put shields up with me anymore, Josephine. Because every time you do, it feels like a stab wound to my heart. And then that makes me put up my shields, and it's all fucking downhill from there."

I stroke his cheek some more. His words should terrify me, only I understand them in an innate, visceral way. Like my soul's naked before him, and somehow, we're already one. Hiding from him under these circumstances would feel like holding my breath or refusing to eat.

I hunch forward to kiss him again, and his left hand comes up, snagging the back of my head and neck as his head turns and his lips capture mine. Passion simmers beneath the surface, making it hard to breathe, and yet his lips feather over mine, teasing and taunting me, drawing me closer. I follow wantonly, no longer caring about the consequences until he claims me with a ferocious masculine authority that catches me off guard.

My brain reels, and I whimper, melting into the warmth of his demanding lips and velvety tongue, which strokes mine with a sensual knowledge that makes me feel every bit of my body all at once, from the shivers running along the length of my spine to the sparks and flames in my toes and the painful throb between my legs.

Pulling back slightly to breathe, I gasp, "I need you, Rock. More than I've ever needed anyone." My voice sounds raw and disembodied, and I almost don't recognize it. "Please don't make me go without you anymore."

His eyes widen, and he smiles in that sexy, relaxed way of his, saying, "I don't want to go without you, either."

"I'm sorry if I sound clingy," I add, knitting my brows.

"You could never be too clingy for me. Not only am I needy as fuck because of my childhood, but now that I've met you, I can't be happy away from you. It feels like a curse until we get together. Then, it feels like bliss."

"Yeah, but I have some serious abandonment issues I should probably warn you about. Past guys I've dated all agree I'm a barnacle."

"A barnacle?" he repeats, raising a questioning eyebrow.

"Clingy AF."

"A barnacle and a rock. Sounds like we were made for each other. You cling to me all you want, Blackbird," he teases, drawing me by my hips to the edge of the tattoo chair so that I feel on the verge of toppling into his lap. He rolls his stool closer, sliding demandingly between my legs.

Chapter Twenty

ROCK

"Tell me what you want from me," I order darkly, knowing by the delicious scent of her arousal what she needs. My hands stroke up and down her legs, my fingers following the lines of her stocking seams. These fucking stockings have my insides on fire.

Her eyes dilate, and her nose flares. Her generous bottom lip trembles at my touch, and her breath comes faster now. "I want you," she replies in hushed tones, the most delicate, feminine creature I've ever seen. I feel torn inside.

The beastly side of me wants to pull her into my lap and fuck the shit out of her. But I know that's not the right approach for handling a virgin. The more calculated side of me wants to take her back to my place and spread her out on the bed, spending hours adoring her body. What if, despite all her clingy talk, she starts panicking again and wants me to take her home without inviting me in?

My cock strains against the inside of my pants zipper, reminding me a cold shower isn't going to cut it this time. Even more than that, though, I'm still fresh off the jealousy of thinking about her with Coolie—intensely aware that if I don't claim her, another man will. That's completely unacceptable.

A middle-ground part of me wants to mark her as mine, possess her in a way that draws nothing from her but heady pleasure and lots of delectable honey. That's the part I decide to go with.

My big, rough hands slide up the length of her legs to the hem of her black pencil skirt, working slowly to inch the stretchy fabric up her thighs. She exhales, her eyes rounding as she watches me, her mouth frozen between speaking and remaining silent.

Keeping my eyes on her, I gently reassure her. "Don't worry, Blackbird. I'm going to make you fly."

"But should we do this here?" she asks, her eyes flickering to the reception area.

"It's just you and me."

"Are you sure about this?"

"Didn't I warn you about what happens to naughty girls who show up at tattoo parlors after dark dressed like pinup presents?"

She whimpers, the pulse point visible in her neck and her tongue wetting her full bottom lip again. What I wouldn't give to stick my cock into that lovely little mouth of hers, feeling her tongue swipe over my head, greedily drawing my cum down her throat. Fuck, I won't be able to hold on if I keep thinking this way.

Despite the concern in her voice, she makes no move to get up or stop my hands. Instead, she watches raptly, her lack of intervention dripping with consent. My hands graze up her legs more urgently now, and when I reach her mid-thighs, I let out an appreciative sigh, realizing she wears garters and thigh highs. *Fuck me.*

"Oh," she says, worrying her bottom lip. "Don't look at my thighs."

"Why not?"

"Because they're fat and bulge over the tops of my stockings."

"I like it," I confess, mesmerized by the plumpness of her lovely stems. All I can think about is getting my head between them and feeling her squeeze the sides of my face.

"And my underwear," she says on a sigh. "Maybe don't look—"

"At the wet spot?" I ask with a wicked grin.

Her face burns as I revel in the beauty of white, lacy underwear with a darker, almost transparent spot, betraying her need. "I love this," I confess, leaning in to smell her heady arousal again. It brings out an animal side of me I can't explain, yearning animating every cell and fiber of my being. I lick the dark spot on the white swatch, getting my first glimmers of her musky flavor.

Effie gasps.

"I need this," I demand, licking the swatch again. "I need to make it mine forever."

"Yes, Rock. I need you so badly, it hurts."

I don't doubt it, looking at that sexy swatch glistening with her honey.

"I can make your pain go away, Blackbird, and replace it with pure ecstasy. Is that what you need?"

"Yes," she sighs, her face burning.

Using my hands, I sweep her legs up overhead, bringing my left hand under her ass and snagging the waistband of her panties. Thanks to my exuberance, I pull them free with more force than I mean to, sending them flying like a stretched rubber band. But I don't give two fucks about finding them now. All I can think about is burying my head in her honeypot.

Throwing one leg over each of my shoulders, I stare at her gorgeous pussy with its immaculately kept landing strip. Fuck,

I wasn't expecting this from a virgin. But then, why not? Everything else about her is kept with meticulous care.

Sweeping my hand up to the top of her pussy, I spread her lips with my first finger and thumb, delighting at the shiny pink perfection that greets me. Her clit pokes out at the top, begging me to devour her, and desire grips me hard. Swallowing to clear the knot in my throat, I ask, "Has a man ever tasted you before, Blackbird?"

She looks down at me, a mixture of curiosity, anticipation, and anxiousness on her face. A shake of her head lets me know I'm the first here, too.

"Good," I say. "Just for the record, I aim to be the first *and* the last." Her face flushes some more, and she smiles at me adoringly.

"Lie back a little, and scoot your ass closer to me," I order, circling her waist with my hands and pulling her to the edge of the seat."

"But I'm going to fall off if you let go of me," she protests breathily.

"I won't ever let go of you," I reply before closing the distance between us with a swipe of my tongue over her pearl...and then another...and another.

Effie pants and moans with each stroke, crazing me to please her. I can't begin to describe how good she tastes. Like a custom-designed flavor made to drive me feral. And her delicious smell has my body alive in every way, ready to devour and fill her with mindless ecstasy.

She leans back, relaxing into the chair some more, and I go to work, sucking and flicking her clit between my teeth. I circle her with my tongue, experimenting with pressure and speed until she sounds like she's hyperventilating. Her thighs tense, and her fingers thread into my hair, holding me in place.

My left hand comes up to her slit, and I slide my thumb back and forth through her juicy edges, already imagining how fucking incredible it'll feel to slide my cock into her messy goodness. She's everything I could ever want. Penetrating her slowly with my pointer finger, I'm amazed at her tightness, wondering in mute shock how I'll ever jam my thick cock inside without splitting her in two.

The last thing I want to do is hurt her. But fuck do I need to be inside that pussy, too. Her walls are already swelling and throbbing with need, and they grip my finger greedily as I curl it back towards me, stimulating the rough spot near the front of her pussy. I work the bundle of nerves as she dissolves around me, panting, fluttering, and drawing tighter and tighter towards her climax.

I love the way she creams my finger, her arousal dripping down my palm and the back of my hand and messing up my tattoo chair. Never in my life have I done this with any woman, though I've certainly had some beg for the experience. But it's not hygienic or professional.

I don't give a fuck about any of this when it comes to Effie, though. I can't wait any longer. This delectable little rockabilly package is all mine, and I mean to unwrap every part of her, stroking her into rapture and marking her as mine.

Her hand presses the back of my head more urgently into her arousal, and she mewls. Her soft, silky pussy walls tighten around my finger, and I add a second, barely able to get it inside her. But I have to make room because I'm on the edge of self-control, and my cock needs her more than I've ever needed any woman.

I'll take her fast, pushing her past the pain quickly so that we can focus on the sensual goodness of being one. For whatever reason, despite my previous concerns, it feels right for me to be the man who takes her virginity. Not that I'm usually into all that traditional, conservative bullshit. But I need her to be mine and mine alone. Lord knows I've already given up enough of her by having other men tattoo her. But that changes tonight.

"Rock," she groans, her breath coming faster, her whimpers trending higher. "Please don't stop!"

Her whole body tenses from her legs to her pussy walls, and I can feel her on the precipice, about to plunge over into pleasure. Fuck, I love being the guy leading her there. With each stroke of my fingers and lap and swirl of my tongue over her pearl, I fall more in love with her until I'm sunk up to my eyeballs in the feeling. There's no fucking escape. I need Effie for all time.

She cries out, bucking her hips as she comes hard, her pussy walls squeezing me in greedy pulses, and her voice piercing the silence with a silky, delectable cry I'll remember for the rest of my life. Her whole body unravels around me, spasming and thrusting upward as euphoria rocks her core, and she grinds her delicious pussy into my face and mouth.

Fuck. Yes.

Pulling my head back, I tap her swollen clit with the forefinger of my free hand, feeling her walls tighten and spasm around me with each drop of my finger. I stop when her breathing slows, pulling my fingers from her and licking them clean. I'm ravenous with need, my cock on high alert.

Chapter Twenty-One

ROCK

"That. Was. Amazing." She pants, her body a pile of relaxed satisfaction, her legs still over my shoulders. Darkly, I say, "We're not done, Blackbird."

"We're not?" she asks, tilting her head forward to look at me.

"No," I reply, shaking my head. "Not even close."

Her eyebrows arch, and her lush pink lips turn up at the edges.

"Sit up, Stormy," I croon softly, and she starts to do so before looking embarrassed.

"But I'll ruin your chair. I'm all...you know."

"Fucking perfect is what you are. To hell with the chair." I guide her legs off my shoulders one at a time before standing to my full height and unbuttoning and unzipping my pants. Effie watches me raptly, her hungry eyes devouring every move I make until I pull the front of my tented boxer briefs down, revealing my thick, large cock.

"That's huge," she exclaims, her eyes rounding. "There's no way..." Effie shakes her head, unable to finish her thought.

I smile, my heart brimming with pride at her observation

and love at her innocence. "Let's give it a try, Blackbird. You're fucking drenched right now, which means I can slide right in." At least, that's the plan. I stroke my cock a couple of times as her eyes take it in. Her face looks both thirsty and terrified.

Reaching into my wallet, I pull out a condom, ripping open the package with my teeth. She watches as I pump my dick a few more times before I slide the thin film down over it to the hilt, her eyes the size of dessert plates.

"I'm clean," I say, my voice raw.

"And I'm clean, too," she says before laughing and catching herself. "I mean, I'm a virgin, so obviously, I'm clean."

"A virgin isn't always clean, Blackbird. That was the right thing to say."

"And I'm not on birth control, so that had better work," she says, pointing at the condom.

"It'll work." I stop myself before adding *they always do*. She doesn't need any comments that remind her of the Lexie situation or that I've been promiscuous as fuck in the past.

The height difference between us requires some managing, so I sit back on the stool, rolling up to her and motioning for her to climb onto my lap. She swallows loudly, her doe eyes large and unblinking as she straddles my lap, sitting a couple inches from my cock. I run the head through her juicy folds, lubing myself in her honey. Fuck it's silky and smooth, and I love covering my cock in her sensual scent, making it clear I'm hers and hers alone.

"I'm going to do this swiftly and decisively. Like tearing off a Band-Aid," I warn her, staring into her beautiful gaze. I'm also going to use gravity to my advantage. "Are you okay with that?"

She bites her bottom lip, and I can tell by the ambivalent look on her face that she struggles with agreeing to something she's never experienced before. I can't blame her. I don't know how else to do this, but she doesn't need to know that either. Despite all my player ways, I've never been with a virgin. Never thought I would be, honestly.

I grab onto her hips with authority as she stands on either side of me, hovering over my rod, her face flooded with concern. "Are you ready for this?" I ask, scrutinizing her expression closely, not only to read her thoughts but to remember for the rest of my life the moment this gorgeous woman gave herself to me for the first time.

"But what if I bleed?" Effie asks quietly. "I don't want to gross you out."

I grin, reaching up to palm her cheek. "There's nothing you could do to gross me out. This is all a natural part of..." I'm about to say having sex, but it's not the right thing to tell her. "This is all a natural part of making love."

"Okay," she says, letting a cute little puff of air escape her lips.

Grabbing her curvy hips with one hand and holding my cock with the other, I guide myself into her pussy, amazed by the tightness. How in the fuck? Even I'm wondering what nature intended. But I don't let on. Instead, I strain to get the tip inside of her as she lets out a little cry, wincing.

"It's too big," she says, breathing hard.

"It's a tight fit," I agree. "And we don't have to get all the way there tonight. But let's see what we can do." I feel more like the big, bad wolf than I ever have in my entire life. But I want to make this good for her, too, which means mastering the situation and figuring this the fuck out. After all, people have been doing this for thousands of years.

Seizing her hips with both hands, I work her down over me demandingly, feeling her grip me so tightly it hurts. Fuck. Yet, I persist, inching my way into her juicy tightness as she squeals and complains about my size. I promised I'd make it quick and decisive, but I'm already fucking up the whole thing.

"Relax," I command gently. "I promise, this won't hurt much longer, and then I'm going to rock your world...in a good way."

Her face grimaces, and her eyelids squeeze firmly together. "Look at me," I order. She doesn't comply, and so I repeat myself all the time, inching deeper into her hot, tight channel. "Effie, look at me..."

She refuses.

"Josephine."

She opens her eyes, staring at my face and instantly relaxing. Good. Spitting on my thumb, I slide my hand between our bodies, finding her swollen nub and circling it with my wet finger. The beauty relaxes some more, all the time gazing at me as my thumb circles her pearl faster and faster, and I slide the tip of my rod in and out of her.

Effie's breathing picks up, and she wraps her arms around my neck, panting next to me so that I feel the heat of her breath on the shell of her ear. Her tight walls grow even tighter around me as she draws closer to her orgasm, and I wait for the perfect moment to make her mine.

She curls her body around me, scratching my back and screaming my name, and I seize the moment. Returning both hands to her hips, I grab her possessively, pulling her completely down over me and breaking through the flap of skin keeping us apart. She screams again but not from pleasure, gasping and searching my face as big, fat teardrops roll down her cheeks. Her expression contains momentary horror like she can't believe I did that to her. And I know now's not the time to stop. I have to push her through all the pain and back onto the road of unabashed enjoyment.

Using my strength, I slide her up and down over my girth, filling her with my rod again and again. Pain transforms into euphoria as her breath synchs with mine, and I stroke her long and hard, possessing her completely and marking her as mine forever.

My eyes meet hers, holding her gaze, and she palms my cheeks, melting into me as I melt into her. There's no delineation between us as I thrust into her again and again, feeling her silky pussy take everything I have to give as she rides me over the edge of rapture again, screaming my name and clawing the hell out of my back with her orgasm. I pound into her, coming so hard fucking stars float around my head.

As the room falls silent, and we continue staring into each other's faces, I can't help myself. "I love you, Josephine," I gasp. "More than I've ever loved any woman. And I'm not saying this because we just had sex. I mean it to the very depths of my soul."

"I love you, too," she whispers, showering my face in tender butterfly kisses as the backs of my eyes sting, and emotion blurs my vision. "It's you and me forever," she says softly.

I hold her against my chest, savoring the feel of her heartbeat and the knowledge she's mine for the long haul. Fuck, it feels good to no longer be alone in this world. To know who my ride or die is and that someone will always have my back, apart from my foster brothers and my dad.

Her body tenses in my arms, her face tightening as she says suddenly, "I'm sorry if that sounded too clingy."

"Not at all, Blackbird. I'm not like other men. I want you to be clingy as fuck, and I want you to want me forever, too," I reassure her, stroking her cheeks and wiping away her tears. "On the lovable days and the unlovable ones. Promise?"

"Promise," she says, smiling as tears fill her eyes, splashing onto her bright pink cheeks.

Chapter Twenty-Two

EFFIE

Watching Rock perform with the Lowlifes is spectacular and bittersweet because it's the end of an era for him. He holds the stage with charisma, not unlike Chris Isaac or a young Elvis Presley. With his updo and Rockabilly outfit, the guitarist and lead singer is mouthwatering, and from the naughty sway of his hips to the snarl of his lips, he's all mine, something he reminds me of every chance he gets.

Even now, with girls screaming his name and performing all sorts of crazy antics to get his attention, he only has eyes for me. As he croons a love song, he stares into the audience, finding me with his gaze and holding on.

We're at the Orpheum in Sacramento, a small downtown theater that's hosted intimate rock concerts since the 1960s psychedelic scene. It's the perfect atmosphere for Dee, who accompanied me to the show. The pragmatic redhead warned me that dealing with Lexie, an inevitability at this concert, is not something she would recommend alone. And I couldn't be more thankful for her presence.

The lanky brunette scowls at me from her seat at the bar,

vacuuming down another shot. With each one, I become more confident she's not pregnant even as I inwardly groan at what her behavior could be doing if she is. After a tense few minutes, she stands, beelining toward me. Dee raises her eyebrows, concerned.

I say resolutely, "I can handle this."

The redhead looks skeptical.

"Just don't stray too far away."

She nods before Lexie towers over me, a sour look on her face. I could get in an actual bar fight tonight with how she's looking at me. "You know who I am, right?" She pronounces the words sloppily.

I nod emphatically, lifting my chin in challenge. "Yes, I know exactly who you are."

"And you know about the baby, right?" Her eyes narrow, and she pats her perfectly flat belly for show. Being a kindergarten teacher comes with many learned skills, including knowing a liar when I see one. From the sudden rapidity of her blinking to how she refuses to make eye contact, I see all the tells that her story is fabricated.

"Yes, I know about everything," I say emphatically. My eyes flicker to the stage, and I see the ambivalence on Rock's face as he watches our interaction. I shoot him a confident smile, letting him know I've got this. Nevertheless, the man's posture tightens, ready to jump off the stage to intervene if needed.

I may be wholesome and sunshiny, but I can throw down with the best of them when needed. Besides, the narcissist reminds me a lot of my own mother, which means I've been custom-tailored my whole life to deal with her.

Lexie's face looks shellshocked, and she staggers back slightly, her sigh shaky. "Wow, you must be desperate. You still want to be with him despite all of this?"

"Yes," I reply firmly. "No matter what comes our way, we'll always be together. Forever."

"That doesn't sound like him," she counters, looking beside herself. "He was never into commitment before."

"Because he had nothing worth committing to," I lob the words at her, preparing to feel a tug on my hair or fingernails in my arm. She looks like the type who will fight dirty. Dee steps closer, her face grim and ready to back me up.

"But I am concerned about you drinking while you're pregnant." I arch my eyebrow. "I wonder what the bartender would think about continuing to serve you tonight?"

She shakes her head, looking irate.

Dee interrogates, "Unless you're not pregnant, Lexie?"

The brunette looks defeated, her shoulders hunching. She directs all her angst at me. "I fucking thought for sure it would break you two up. You little slut. Goddammit! No, I'm not pregnant, but you're going to regret being with Rock. He'll fucking cheat on you the first chance he gets. All bad-boy rockers are the same."

I cock my head to the side, working hard to control the vindication I feel inside. "You let me worry about that. Besides, you've got plenty of answering to do for your lies. How do you think Bub will feel about finding out you're not actually pregnant? Or even worse, thinking you'd be so irresponsible with alcohol if you were?"

"That's none of your damn business," she hisses, stepping closer.

Dee intercedes. "You've said more than enough tonight, Lexie. Time to back the fuck up before I get security involved." The redhead's eyes shoot behind us. When I turn, I see a bouncer nodding towards her. "Want to try me?"

Lexie exhales sharply, red-faced and steaming. Turning on her heels, she storms through the crowd out the bar's front doors. My eyes follow her until she disappears outside.

I look at Dee, and she breathes a sigh of relief. Fisting her knuckle, she says matter-of-factly, "I was starting to think I'd have to make use of all my rings tonight."

I grimace at the thought of her punching Lexie with enough decorative rings to form makeshift brass knuckles. "I'm glad it didn't come to that."

"And I'm glad we got a little clarity. I never thought Lexie was pregnant. As you can see, she's quite the drama queen."

I sigh, relief washing over me. As much as I was prepared to step up and help Rock with a baby, I didn't want to consider the infant's health with the way Lexie throws back at the bar. It's one less concern we have to worry about.

It's been a week since we got together at the tattoo parlor, and Rock's been a man of his word when it comes to being clingy. He moved me and the kittens into his cabin that night, doubling up on the bottles of Calamine.

Dee stepped in the next day, offering to foster the kittens. With any luck, they'll become a regular feature of the cafe. I've even joked with her she needs to change the name to Three Cats Cafe.

Dee leans towards me, whispering, "By the way, you and Rock make the cutest couple. I knew you were perfect for each other the night you came into the romance readers group talking about tattooed cowboys. Remember that?"

I nod, giggling. "Yes, I do."

"But then getting to know you and hearing you sing. You two are made for each other—"

Dee's whisper comes to a halt as Rock looks out at me, furrowing his brow and saying, "Blackbird, are you ready to perform a couple of numbers with me?" He shields his eyes from the spotlights with his hand, pointing in my direction.

"Oh, boy," I say shakily to Delilah

The redhead squeezes my hand. "You're going to do great."

I nod uncertainly, picking my way up to the front of the theater and climbing the stairs to the stage. When I reach Rock, he wraps his arm possessively around my waist, leaning down for a passionate kiss that gets the crowd roaring and the girls screaming. I don't know if it's with joy or rage.

Smiling broadly, he says, "This here's the love of my life, Ms. Josephine Jackson. She's the June Carter to my Johnny Cash, the Wanda Jackson to my Elvis, and the barnacle to my rock."

I swat his shoulder playfully, and he laughs deep in his throat. "She's my everything. Would you like to hear this songbird and I sing a few numbers?"

The crowd goes wild, and my heart flip-flops in my chest like a fish out of water. My cheeks burn, and my pulse drums in my temples. Looking up at Rock, dazed by the lights, terror grips me, and I can't remember what we're singing. He hands me my guitar, and it feels foreign in my hands. The lyrics to come evaporate from my head. I'll never know how this man has spent years of his life doing this for a living.

The room is deathly quiet as the lights draw down, giving us a few minutes to tune. Instead, he pulls me close, whispering, "I saw Lexie giving you a hard time. Are you okay?"

I exhale sharply. "She's not pregnant. She admitted it to Dee and me."

The muscle in his jaw jumps, but his expression never wavers. "I always thought that was the case. But how'd you get her to admit it?"

"I told her the truth. That I'll stick by you no matter what happens in this world. You're my ride or die."

A big smile captures his face, and he leans down, kissing me again, careful to keep our guitars from smashing together. "I love you, Blackbird," he whispers.

"I love you, too," I reply, my face taut with adrenaline and anxiety.

Chapter Twenty-Three

EFFIE

"What else is wrong, Effie?"

I confess breathily, "It's too many lights. Too many people. I'm afraid I'll mess up."

"That's not possible with me. Whatever you do is exactly what you're supposed to. Rock pulls back slightly, staring earnestly into my eyes. "Just look at me, Effie, and remember I will love you until I draw my last breath. And after that, too, God willing."

I take a stilted inhale and then another as he motions for the band to start playing behind us, and the lights come back up. Rock smiles warmly. As the music washes over me, my fingers relax on my guitar strings, sliding over chords. Lyrics wash over me, and I give Rock a firm nod, telling him I'm ready. Only then does Rock launch into "Twisted Games."

I keep my eyes on him the whole time, cycling through the playlist we've grown accustomed to from playing together in Hollister. "Ring of Fire," "Suspicious Minds," "Between the Bars." We finish with "Happy Trails," the perfect song to conclude the first half of the Lowlifes concert. As we head backstage for intermission, Rock and I put our guitars away before he grabs my hand, saying, "There are a couple of guys I'd like you to meet."

I nod, smoothing my slate gray pencil skirt and making sure none of the tiny buttons on my black sweater set with embroidered roses on the neckline have come undone. He leads me to a dressing room door, standing outside and explaining, "I reached out to your mother to get her here tonight. But she couldn't make it. She called at the last minute...something to do with a guy named Fred."

I frown. Still on that. Ugh!

"But I've got two guys here dying to meet you." He stares at me thoughtfully for a moment. Taking a deep breath, he says, "Promise me, no matter what happens, you won't get too mad at me."

"What?" I arch my eyebrows quizzically.

Rock opens his mouth to speak, but the door swings open before us. An impatient-looking man with clean-cut brown hair motions for us to enter the room. "I thought I heard your fucking voice, you fucking, motherfucker."

My eyes round.

Rock laughs, pointing at the man. "This is my music producer, Steve Harley."

"Call me Skates," the man says impatiently, grabbing my hand and shaking hard.

I smile, uncertain what I think of the brash guy.

"You and I are in for a talk tonight. I've already got this guy semi onboard," he says, nodding towards Rock. "Now it's time to get buy-in from you on those fucking amazing duets."

My heart jumps in my chest. Rock confessed to me before tonight's show that he secretly recorded a demo tape and sent it to his music producer. But the moment still feels surreal, and I'm unsure how to process it. After all, I spent my whole life fixated on the evils of the rock star lifestyle. The idea of becoming a professional performer myself twists my stomach.

Rock wraps his arm back around me, pulling me into the room where a second, much shorter man stands further back, tears flooding his eyes. I would recognize those long salt and pepper dreadlocks reaching his mid-back anywhere. Heck, anybody would. His powder blue eyes absorb me quietly, and his face is softer and shyer than I would imagine. Of course, I've only ever seen photos and videos of him performing with Scared and Dazed as lead singer.

"Wow, just wow!" he says quietly, taking me in for a long moment. His eyes have a tenderness to them that I wasn't expecting. Of course, I was never expecting to meet him at all.

"Sax Gunner," I say quietly, the corners of my mouth turning down slightly. I bite my lower lip hard, realizing all eyes are on me and him...my long-lost father.

"You have quite a voice," he says quietly, the tears spilling over his eyes and down his cheeks. "I told myself I wouldn't do this. But until a few days ago, I didn't even know you existed."

My brows knit. "That's not true," I say quietly, shaking my head. "Mom said you knew all about me and didn't want anything to do with me. That you were just an irresponsible rocker bad boy like all the rest."

"No," he says quietly, shaking his head and sighing. "That story doesn't surprise me, though. Joann always manipulated circumstances to suit her needs. I'm sorry to say that because I know she's your mother. But sadly, she didn't tell me about you at all. Instead, she disappeared with the next musician who caught her fancy. I'm not sure I would believe this, except you look so much like my mother." More tears wet his cheeks as he steps forward slowly.

I don't even realize I'm crying until he tentatively reaches his hands up to my face, wiping away my tears. It's the kind of gesture I've seen a million times on TV when a father comforts his daughter after she skins her knee or falls from a bike. But I gave up long ago on expecting this from my father.

I don't even realize how much I need this man to hug me until I reach out my arms, and he holds me, stroking my hair and telling me how thankful he is to know that I exist. That it's the most beautiful news he's had in a very, very long time, and he wants to do what he can to make up for lost time if I let him be a part of my life.

Rock stands a distance away, talking with Skates, eyeing me affectionately. I smile broadly at him, and his shoulders relax a little bit. There's no way I could be mad at him for this amazing moment.

Sax motions for me to sit down on the couch next to him, asking about my life, my career, and how I started singing with Rock. The story of the dead man in the bush makes him laugh until he cries.

The rock legend wants to know everything. And unlike my mom, who goes through question-asking like it's rote without actually listening to my answers, he contemplates my every word with sensitivity, asking for clarification where appropriate, and nodding as he processes it all.

I don't know how much time passes before Rock says, "I've got to go back onstage. The crowd's about to rip the place apart. Are you good, Blackbird?" He points at Sax and me.

I nod.

Skates heads in my direction, but Rock grabs his arm. "No pressuring my girl without me around. Leave these two alone. They've got plenty of catching up to do." He drags the reluctant producer through the door with him, shutting it behind us.

Sax smiles, an undeniable kindness written on his face. "You have a good man there. I'd take him for a son-in-law any day. And he's really worked overtime to make this meeting happen." Lifting his hand, he palms my cheek, more tears filling his eyes. "I am so proud of you, and I want to know everything about your life and what you've been up to all these years. I also want you to meet my wife and your younger siblings. You have two younger brothers and two younger sisters."

My head reels at the found family he's offering as tears cascade down my cheeks. To go from lonely to a whole family in the blink of an eye is difficult to grasp. But I can tell by the warmth in his eyes that he has nothing but the best intentions for getting to know me.

Epilogue

EFFIE

SIX WEEKS LATER

I've got a blindfold over my eyes, and Rock holds my hand, leading me from the bedroom of our cabin down the hallway toward the living room.

"Can I look yet?" I ask impatiently.

The big cowboy changes his tack. Instead of leading me, he comes up behind me, wrapping his big arms around me so my arms are pinned at my sides, carrying me the rest of the way. "No peeking!" he scolds against the shell of my ear, shedding his hot breath on my cheek and making my lower core tighten with need. I can never get enough of this guy, even though we spent most of the day in bed making love slowly and sensually before the doorbell rang, and he ran out in his boxers to get my surprise delivered to the house.

He sets my bare feet back on the wood floor, grabbing my hand and guiding me to sit down.

"Are you ready for your Valentine's—"

A tiny "meow" fills the air, and before he can stop me, I remove the blindfold, staring at two small, hairless kittens. I can't help but laugh, my eyes ticking towards Rock, who scrutinizes my reaction quietly.

They each have large bluish-gray eyes, and their tiny bodies are covered in dusty gray Siamese markings. "Oh, my goodness! They're adorable!" I exclaim, grabbing them one at a time and plopping them into my lap. I marvel at their warm little bodies and velvety softness, stroking and playing with them.

Rock's eyes glint with happiness, a satisfied smile capturing his lips. To my shock, he grabs the one closest to him, holding it gently in his big, rough hands.

"But you're allergic. Aren't you going to break out in hives or something?" That's the last thing we need, considering we have a concert tonight in Ophir City.

"So, this breed is called a Sphynx cat, and while no feline is completely hypoallergenic, these hairless buggers come pretty damn close. And I've got Calamine in the medicine cabinet if I still end up being allergic to them."

"I love them so much." I lean forward, kissing the cowboy. "Thank you, baby."

"I reached out to a well-established breeder. She's the president of the Sphynx Feline Association. I got to meet the parents, see these guys and their littermates on and off over the past eight weeks, and spend plenty of time holding and getting to know the breed. I have yet to break out in a rash. Fingers crossed."

"How did you find time to do all of this?" I ask, amazed.

"Easy now that I'm only allowed to tattoo fifty percent of humanity," he laughs, referring to my rule that he not tattoo women. "And with the Lowlifes calling it quits, I have a lot more free time. By the way, we have a little boy and a girl here. I say we name them Elvis and Wanda," Rock says, smiling at me. "Thoughts?"

I clap my hands together, excited. "That's perfect! Just like their Mama and Daddy."

Rock lies on his side on the rug, the kittens batting around his naked torso. He wears nothing but boxer briefs, perfectly showing off his rock-hard physique and tattoos. Ink covers him from head to toe—an eagle, nautical star, shellback turtle, rooster, pig, octopus, squid, mermaid, swallows, hula girl, pinup girls, fully rigged ship, and more. Some pieces commemorate his time in the Navy like when he crossed the equator for the first time, went through the Panama Canal, and entered various ports. Some have to do with traditional sailor superstitions. All of them turn me on to no end.

Interspersing the vintage work are gorgeous, hyperrealistic portraits, including images of his foster dad and mom in their youth. Over the past six weeks, I've spent countless hours tracing each tattoo with my fingers, asking him about their meaning, and teasing my way into plenty of sexy time.

He looks at me now, laughing at the kittens' antics. The long, slanting rays of the sun grab my attention. Glancing at the clock, I say breathlessly, "It's already five. We have to get ready for our concert."

Sadly, the performance where I met Sax Gunner was Rock and the Lowlifes' last gig. I feel robbed that I didn't get to see more of his concerts with the group. But after facing off against Lexie, she worked viciously behind Rock's back to finish off the group. Fortunately, between tattooing and honing our duets, he hasn't acted fazed by the close of this chapter in his life. If anything, he's relieved.

We're playing a Valentine's Concert at the Melodeon, a Gold Rush-era theater in Ophir City with a quaint historical vibe. To my surprise, the last time Rock checked, the concert was sold out, making my nerves spike every time I think about it.

But Rock wants to get a few performances under our belts

before we head into the recording studio with Skates later this month. The studio's located in Los Angeles, and we'll be staying with Sax Gunner and his family in a guest house on their oceanfront property in Newport Beach. He insisted, anxious for me to meet his wife, Cindy, and my younger brothers and sisters.

It's all a lot to take in and slightly overwhelming. But Rock is with me every step of the way, my anchor and my steady presence no matter what.

We won't go on stage until after eight tonight, but if Rock's hellbent on pomading his hair, it will take a while. Like a long while. I joke it takes longer for him to get ready than me, and I have documented evidence to prove it.

Jumping to his feet as lithely as the morning I caught him in my bushes, he grabs my hand, leading me down the hallway. "Are you going to wear your seamed stockings, Blackbird?"

I nod, smiling. "I was planning on wearing a dress tonight."

"Mmm..." he growls deep in his throat. "What would I have to do to talk you into putting on your stockings, garters, and corset and then sitting on my face?"

I gasp at his naughty suggestion, taken aback daily by something the sexy bad-boy cowboy suggests. "You're incorrigible, Rockwell Landry. Besides, we'll be late if—"

"But it'll help with my stage fright," he teases, wrapping his arm around my waist and lifting me off the ground to carry me down the hallway. Irrepressible giggles overtake me as we reach the bedroom, and he adds, "I refuse to go onstage until I get a mouthful of that sweet pussy. Do it for our fans, Blackbird."

"Not on your life," I say, turning and looking him in the face. My cheeks flush. "But I will do it to help with *my* stage fright."

He chuckles seductively. "Not only will my tongue guarantee you're relaxed and happy tonight during the performance, but if I have my way, you'll be purring like my little sex kitten, too."

～

Rock's attempts at warming me up to live performances are working. Although I'm used to the Mommy and Me Saturday morning shows that Alex and I still do religiously, the lights of a stage and the massive crowds still make my heart race and my palms sweaty. But my hands shake less this time, which is a welcome relief for a guitar player.

Looking to the right, I eye Rock's entire family in the box seat next to the stage. Everyone's here except for the kids who Stacey, a former waitress at the Silver Fork, babysits. She's now one of Dee's employees.

In December, her boss, Jerry Lee, disappeared into thin air after a blizzard. Apparently, they had a thing going because she's been bereft ever since, even begging Rock to give her a small tattoo on her wrist to commemorate her former boss.

It's one of the weirdest stories I've ever heard, and it saddens Dee to no end. She and Jerry were close. Heck, it saddens all of us because Hollister isn't the same without Jerry and the Silver Fork. And Stacey walks through life like a half-person these days. But she's great with kids and seems to want to stay extra busy, making her the perfect person for the job.

Rock strums the familiar opening chords of "Twisted Games," and we launch into our set. My eyes dart between my singing partner and the box seat, trying not to focus on the crowd.

That's what Rock told me to do...focus on my family, those who love me the most. Before Christmas Eve, I believed that was one fly-by-night person—my mom. My heart fills to bursting thinking about all that Rock's brought into my life, and I have to stop thinking about this or risk bursting into tears.

Besides, the crowd has the crying handled for us. Between our melding voices, acoustic chords, and Alex's cello accompaniment, there are few dry eyes in the room by the end, and poor Jess has tears streaming down her face. She's so pregnant at this point that her stomach looks like it could pop, and Logan has his arm protectively around her at all times.

By the show's end, the crowd cheers and stands, begging for encores. Rock told me to anticipate this, so we go through the three extra songs we planned. But when he steps towards the mic to play a fourth, I eye him in mute horror. I have no idea what he's doing.

He smiles mischievously. "You can put your guitar down for this one, Blackbird, and have a seat."

I can barely blink before a stagehand appears, taking my guitar. My eyes round, and I feel naked onstage, perched on my stool.

Rock leans into the mic, "That was some show, huh?"

The crowd cheers and cheers until he has to motion for them to quiet down. "I've got one more," he says, side-eyeing me. "A little number I'm dedicating to my adorable singing partner. For your love for me and standing with me forever, despite drama, angst, rumors, you name it. I hope you like it. Here it goes."

My heart slams against my chest as his fingers pick the beautiful acoustic melody to Elvis Presley's "Can't Help Falling in Love," accompanied by lush, low notes from Alex's cello. I look back at her, raising an eyebrow, and she shrugs and smiles. They've been working on this together for a while now. Rock knows this is my all-time favorite love song.

Tears flow down my face as he croons the tune, and the audience listens breathlessly. By the end, I'm sure most of my mascara drips from my chin, but he doesn't look phased as he reaches into his pocket, producing a small black velvet box. "Ms. Josephine Avery Jackson, would you do me the honor of becoming my wife?"

The crowd bursts into applause and cheers, and I don't hesitate, answering breathlessly. "Yes, one hundred percent. Forever."

Leaning into the mic for the crowd, his voice floods with joy as he confirms with an ear-to-ear grin, "She said 'yes,' folks." They break into exuberant applause. Rock barely gets his guitar strap over his head before I reach him, wrapping my arms around him. He leans into me, whispering against the shell of my ear. "No woman has ever made me feel happier or more complete. And I'd die without you."

I pull back slightly, looking into his sensitive, expressive eyes. For all the melodrama of his words, the rocker's telling me the truth. "And I could never stand to live without you," I reply as he claims my mouth, sweeping me backward to the audience's raucous applause.

Scuttling me offstage, he pulls me towards the dressing room we used earlier. "But shouldn't we go back out? They're still applauding."

"Fuck 'em," he says darkly. "I need to be alone with my future wife."

My breath catches in my throat, uncertain of what he means. This theater doesn't strike me as the most private place. He closes the door, seizing me in his arms and kissing me passionately. Pressing me tightly against him, I can feel the firm outline of his rod on my stomach, and my panties go instantly damp.

When he finally pulls back, letting me breathe, I gasp, "Thank you, baby."

"For what, Blackbird?"

"For making me the happiest woman on this planet. For taking me out of a lonely, sad life and surrounding me with more family than I could ever imagine. I don't just mean Sax Gunner. I mean your foster brothers and their wives and children. Dad and Uncle Billy—"

A knock sounds on the dressing room door, and Rock frowns, annoyance washing over his face. "What?" he calls.

The door opens slowly, and Lily and Turner peer in. The handsome cowboy drawls, "First off, congratulations. That was some show and some proposal, you two. Good luck with this one, Effie. He's trouble."

"All you Rough & Ready boys are," Lily chimes in, swatting Turner's shoulder playfully.

The cowboy adds, "Secondly, it's go-time, folks."

Rock and I both stare at him, puzzled.

Lily explains, "Jess went into labor during the second half of the concert. "So, everyone's meeting at the hospital. We'll see you there." The couple hurries away, shutting the door behind them.

"Dang," Rock says, a big smile lighting him up from ear to ear.

"You already look the part of the proud uncle," I laugh, side-eyeing him.

"I am. Believe me. But I'm also looking forward to the day when it's me taking you to the hospital to have our first child."

"Really?" I ask. "That doesn't sound like much of a rock star plan. And it doesn't really fit with Skate's plans for us recording and going on the road."

My tattooed cowboy sighs. "As much as I love singing with you, I want a real life with you, Blackbird. I want deep roots. Not a subsistence on the road. Between my time in the Navy and my years in the Lowlifes, I've spent much of my adult life wandering. I'm tired of putting off my life to ramble. Will I love recording with you in the studio? Absolutely. Am I willing to tour with you? On and off, for sure. But even more than that, I'm chomping at the bit to play house with you,

Mama. Call it what you will. The rock-star bad boy tamed into a family man. It happened to old Sax Gunner, and now it's happened to me."

"Sax did go on and on about what a great guy you are and how much he'd love having you as his son-in-law. You'd think you paid him to say all that stuff."

Rock laughs, "No, Ma'am, but Josephine Landry has a nice ring to it. Don't you think?"

Staring down at the sparkly, heart-shaped diamond on my left hand, tears splatter my cheeks, "It has the best ring to it because it makes you and me family forever, and nobody can take that away from us."

"Happy Valentine's Day," he says, enveloping me in his arms and kissing me breathless again.

"Happy Valentine's Day," I pant. "Ready to become an uncle and aunt together?"

He nods firmly, palming my cheek and adding with a look of pure adoration, "And husband and wife and Mama and Daddy. I've got big plans for you, Blackbird, and singing duets is only a tiny, beautiful fraction of that. Now, what do you say we get over to the hospital and welcome a new member of the family?"

"Yes, baby," I smile broadly, overwhelmed by the beauty of the future before us.

Can't get enough of Effie and Rock? Read an exclusive bonus scene at this link: https://www.engrideaves.com/freebies/

Thirsting for more steamy romance featuring a grumpy, OTT, possessive alpha mountain man and a sassy, curvy girl?

Ridge is a wild outdoorsman who goes viral with survival videos. Paige is a TV show producer determined to make him famous. But first, she has to tame him without falling for his wild ways...

Discover the next steamy installment of the Rough & Ready Country series, *Love at First Wild:* https://www.engrideaves.com/love-at-first-wild/

Or explore the Rough & Ready Country series. Available now in KU: https://amzn.to/40MMGoa

～

Jonesing to find out what happens when Fierce Amestoy finally meets up with Felicity, his "mountain mate"? Read *Forever with the Mountain Man*, a part of the Mountain Man Mail Order Bride series: https://a.co/d/7pwuuw5.

～

Ready for the full scoop on Stacey and Jerry Lee, the owner of the Silver Fork who mysteriously vanishes? Read *Mountain Man Santa*, part of the Naughty & Spice series: https://www.engrideaves.com/naughty-spice-christmas/

Also by Engrid Eaves

ROUGH & READY COUNTRY

Love at First Blizzard - He's a reclusive mountain man who runs a husky rescue, but his world gets turned upside down by the curvy classical musician he saves from a freak March blizzard.

Love at First Campfire - She's a headstrong, curvy true crime reporter who's never needed anybody until a handsome search and rescue unit lead risks everything to save her.

Love at First Rescue - He's a small-town sheriff who plays by the rules until his sexy dispatcher changes up the game, initiating a rescue that sets long-time passions ablaze.

Love at Second Chance - She's the new home health nurse in Rough & Ready Country, but miles of history with the grumpy ranch foreman are in danger of reigniting, despite her best intentions.

Love at First Baby - He's a wildland firefighter who refuses to settle down for anyone until the curvy hometown sweetheart and an unexpected baby make him reconsider what and who he's living for.

Love and Forgiveness - She's a museum director trying to move on until her estranged husband's security company wins her facility's contract, resurrecting long-buried passions.

Love at First Relationship - Everything about Flynn's paralegal, Jasmine, is off-limits as his much younger, inexperienced employee. But a fake relationship proposal quickly blossoms into much more.

Love at First House - A marriage of convenience is the only way to help Turner's neighbor keep her family together. He tells himself it's a practical arrangement, but his heart has other plans.

Love at First Night - He's a helicopter pilot crushing on his best friend's little sister, Roxy. A cataclysmic night gives them a glimmer into a world of possibilities, but will love or heartbreak prevail?

Love at First Beat - Army cardiologist, Fletcher, excels at healing... But matters of the heart are another thing. Until he meets Drew, a romance writer, who specializes in happy endings.

Love at First Doubt - Kindergarten teacher, Effie, knows the town bad boy, Rock, is trouble. A tattoo artist and rockabilly musician, the cowboy's all wrong for the wholesome curvy girl. Or is he?

Love at First Wild - Ridge is a wild outdoorsman mountain man who goes viral with survival videos. Paige is a TV show producer determined to make him famous. But first, she has to tame him...

Love at First Secret

Love at First Revenge

Love and Redemption

ROUGH & READY LAWMEN

Possessed by the Bounty Hunter - A six-figure bounty draws me back to my ex-fiancée and her mafia-linked Creole family. Soon, a centuries-old curse blurs the line between hunter and hunted.

LOG CABIN CHRISTMAS

Gifted to the Mountain Man - Farzad's first Christmas stateside is lonely until the woman he can't stop thinking about needs protection. As sparks fly, will his cabin and heart be big enough for two?

NAUGHTY & SPICE

Mountain Man Santa - A blizzard leaves Jerry snowed in with his curvy server, Stacey. She may not be ready for commitment...or the secrets of his dark past. But naughty or nice, he won't stop until she's all his...

About the Author

Engrid Eaves publishes short, sweet, and steamy romances featuring gruff alpha male protectors and the headstrong, curvy girls they fall head over heels for.

Her heroes may have painful pasts, but they always find forever with their soulmates. Sexy, satisfying, heartfelt happily ever afters guaranteed!

If you'd like to stay in touch or get your next delicious cowboy mountain man, curvy girl romance fix (and who doesn't?), sign up for her newsletter: www.engrideaves.com.

goodreads.com/engrideaves

bookbub.com/profile/engrid-eaves

instagram.com/engrid_eaves

tiktok.com/@authorengrideaves

facebook.com/EngridEavesAuthor

www.ingramcontent.com/pod-product-compliance
Lightning Source LLC
Chambersburg PA
CBHW032213190626
46810CB00019B/3032